W9-CRG-130

Congratulations on your Baptism. Wishing you the best of Love !!

LienAnh Mai & Family

11/18/2011

Cover illustrated by Jan Folletta
Back cover illustrated by Carolyn Croll

Copyright © 2006 Publications International, Ltd.
All rights reserved.

This publication may not be reproduced in whole or in part
by any means whatsoever without written permission from

Louis Weber, C.E.O.
Publications International, Ltd.
7373 North Cicero Avenue
Lincolnwood, Illinois 60712

Ground Floor, 59 Gloucester Place
London W1U 8JJ

Customer Service: 1-800-595-8484 or customer_service@pilbooks.com

www.pilbooks.com

Permission is never granted for commercial purposes.

p i kids is a registered trademark of Publications International, Ltd.

8 7 6 5 4 3 2 1

ISBN-13: 978-0-7853-6296-8
ISBN-10: 0-7853-6296-7

5-MINUTE BIBLE STORIES

publications international, ltd.

CONTENTS

CONTENTS

CONTENTS

CREATION

Adapted by Brian Conway

Illustrated by Claudine Gévry

In the beginning, there was nothing, only darkness all around. And there was God. God created the heavens and the earth. But the earth was empty and dark. God had a plan to give it shape and life.

"Let there be light," God said. A warm brightness filled the earth. This was light. God called the light "day." He called the darkness "night." This was the first day.

On the second day, God said, "Let there be a great space." A great space surrounded the earth. By day it was a bright blue. By night it was a dark black. God called this great space "sky."

On the third day, God said, "Let the waters flow upon the earth, and let dry ground appear." The water formed oceans and rivers, lakes and ponds. The ground formed mountains and valleys, deserts and islands. God planted trees, grass, and flowers. He gave these plants seeds, so they could bear fruit and grow.

God looked upon what he had created and was pleased.

On the fourth day, God looked into the empty sky and said, "Let there be lights in the sky." God created two great lights and hung them in the sky. He called the brighter light "sun." He made the sun shine over the world during the day. The other light he called "moon." The moon gave the dark night sky a soft, cool glow. Then God added small, sparkling stars to shimmer in the darkness of night.

On the fifth day, God looked into the seas. He said, "Let the waters be alive with creatures." To the great expanses of water, God added creatures of all sizes, shapes, and colors.

Then God looked again into the big blue skies. He said, "Let the skies be alive with creatures that fly." God made creatures with wings, which he called "birds." The birds flew playfully across the great spaces of the sky.

God looked upon all that he had created. The land, the plants, the flowing waters, the sky, the creatures of the seas, the creatures of the skies — they were all good. And God was pleased.

On the sixth day, God said, "Let there be creatures to live upon the land." God created all the animals that roam the earth. Some were small, others were tall. Some lived in the ground, others stayed in the trees. Some had short fur, others were shaggy. Some could walk, others would creep along the earth. Some were loud, others were quiet. Some moved quickly, others moved slowly.

In the fields, God placed cows and sheep, horses and buffalo, rabbits and mice. Soon the woods were filled with scurrying squirrels and chipmunks, fast foxes and deer, creeping spiders, and insects so small that no one but God could see them.

The jungles came alive with fierce tigers, chattering chimpanzees, slithering snakes, and trumpeting elephants. There were animals with long necks and others with stripes and spots. There were animals who came out only at night, and animals who would sleep all winter.

God created so many animals. Every animal was special in its own way. God wanted all of the creatures to grow and have children.

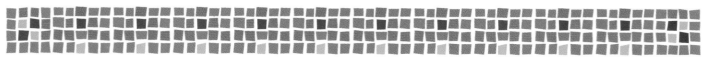

And God created another creature on that sixth day. This creature would also live on land. He called this creature "man."

Man was created in God's own image. God placed man on the earth to watch over all living things — the fish in the sea, the birds in the sky, and the animals on the land.

God blessed this first man. He said to him, "Grow in this place that I have made for you. Take the plants that grow on the land. They will be food for you. Share this land and its food with all the creatures of the world. Live upon this world I have created for you. Make sure that all the world's creatures multiply and prosper."

The man had received God's blessing over all living things.

This is how God created the world from nothing. From darkness, he created light. From emptiness, he created life.

Each thing that God created was good, and he was pleased.

God created day and night, earth and sky, sun and moon, land and sea. He made the plants that grow, the fish that swim, the birds that fly, and the animals that roam. God created a man to watch over the world he had made.

From the heavens, God looked upon his creation. He saw that it was very good.

God blessed the seventh day and made it holy. On the seventh day, when God's wonderful work was done, he rested.

ADAM AND EVE

Adapted by Lora Kalkman

Illustrated by Karen Pritchett

In the beginning, God created the heavens and the earth. Then he created trees and flowers and plants. He created birds and fish and animals. Then God created Adam, the first man.

God wanted Adam to be happy, so he created a glorious garden where Adam could live. It was called the Garden of Eden. God filled the garden with everything Adam could ever want or need.

The Garden of Eden was the most beautiful place on earth. It was filled with tall trees that provided shade and bright flowers that made the garden smell lovely. It was filled with clear brooks where fish swam. When Adam was thirsty, he could cup his hands and drink the cool water. The garden also was filled with all sorts of plants with delicious foods for Adam to eat. Adam was very pleased with his home.

One day, God brought all of the creatures of the earth to the garden so Adam could name them. There were tigers and monkeys, birds and butterflies. There were so many magnificent animals, and Adam happily named each one.

Adam enjoyed his lovely home and all of his animal friends. Still, God could see that Adam was lonely. God decided to make a partner for Adam. One day, when Adam was asleep, God performed a miracle. He took one rib from Adam's chest, and with it, he created a woman. The woman's name was Eve.

Adam loved Eve very much. Eve was Adam's friend and his helper. Adam and Eve were married in the lovely Garden of Eden.

Adam and Eve enjoyed living in the garden. God saw that Adam and Eve were very happy, which pleased him. In exchange for all he gave them, God expected the couple to follow just one simple rule.

"You may eat from any tree in the garden, except the Tree of the Knowledge of Good and Evil," God said.

Adam and Eve did not question God. They were grateful to God, and they wanted to obey God's command. Adam and Eve wanted nothing more than to live happily in the beautiful garden forever.

One day, Adam and Eve walked by the Tree of the Knowledge of Good and Evil. Eve noticed the big red apples dangling from its branches. The apples looked delicious, but Eve remembered God's command not to eat from that tree.

Just then, a long green snake slithered along a branch toward Eve. The snake wanted to tempt Eve into disobeying God's rule.

"Eve," the sly snake hissed, "why don't you pick some apples from this tree? They are bigger and sweeter than any others, I promise you."

"Oh, no," Eve replied. "God told us not to eat from this tree."

"But if you eat these apples, you will become as smart as God," the snake said.

Eve wanted to be very smart. She picked two apples from the forbidden tree. She took a bite from one apple and gave the other to Adam. He also took a bite of the apple, though he knew he should not.

God went to the garden. Adam and Eve tried to hide from him. Adam and Eve hid because they were ashamed that they had disobeyed God. God then realized that they had eaten from the forbidden tree. God was not angry, but he was very sad.

God had no choice but to punish Adam, Eve, and the snake for breaking his rule. He forced the snake to slither on the ground forever. He made the snake an enemy to men and women.

"The snake will now be able to bite and poison people," God said. "And people will now step on the snake."

Then God told Adam and Eve they would have to leave. He said, "Now you will have to plant your own garden and grow your own food. You will have to work hard to build a new home to protect yourselves from the rain and cold."

God gave Adam and Eve clothing made from animal skins. Then he sent them away from the Garden of Eden forever.

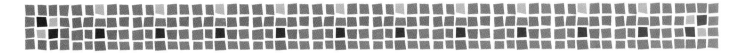

God watched in sorrow as Adam and Eve walked away. He knew that Adam and Eve would grow tired from cutting and hauling wood to build their house. He knew they would be hungry when there was not enough rain to make their garden grow. This made God sad, for even though Adam and Eve had disobeyed him, God still loved them.

Once Adam and Eve had gone, God asked some angels in heaven to guard his precious garden. The angels were happy to serve God, and they flew to earth to protect the Garden of Eden. Because Adam and Eve had broken God's rule, sadly, they were never able to return to the garden again.

NOAH'S ARK

Adapted by Suzanne Lieurance

Illustrated by Carolyn Croll

Once, long ago, the earth had become a very bad place. People were hurting each other, and no one was obeying God. God was disappointed. He decided the world needed a new beginning.

Noah, his wife, and their three sons were good people. The sons were married to good women. God knew that Noah and his family would listen to him, so he trusted them with a very serious job.

God told Noah that a flood would soon cover the earth with water. He told Noah to build a boat for himself and his family. This boat, called an ark, would have to be big enough to save Noah, all of his family, and a pair of every kind of animal in the world, too!

God promised Noah that he and his family would be safe inside the ark. God told Noah to trust him.

Noah listened carefully to God, as he always did, then started to build the ark. His sons helped him, and his wife and his sons' wives filled the ark with everything they would need to survive.

Noah and his family worked and worked. It took them a long time to build the ark, but finally they finished it. Noah and his family were almost ready for the storm.

The sky slowly darkened, and soon there was a long line of animals parading toward the ark. The animals lined up, two by two, with a male and a female of each kind of animal ready to board the ark. Pairs of zebras and giraffes and elephants lined up. Rabbits, horses, and turtles lined up. Lions, monkeys, and dogs stood in line, too.

Noah watched the clouds gather as he stood at the door of the ark. "Welcome," Noah said to each of the animals as they entered the ark. "We must hurry. The storm is coming."

The animals moved faster and quickly came aboard, but many still stood impatiently in line. Looking into the darkening skies, Noah's wife worried that it might be too late.

"God told me to trust him," Noah said. "He will protect us."

At last, when all the animals had entered, Noah and his family boarded the ark. Noah pulled up the plank and sealed the door shut just as it began to rain.

First, only tiny drops of water fell, but soon sheets of rain pelted the ark. The ground quickly turned to mud. The mud quickly became big puddles. The puddles quickly became ponds and then lakes.

It rained and rained. It rained for forty days and forty nights. Water covered everything. There was no land anywhere. Even the mountains were covered with water. But Noah, his family, and all the animals were safe and dry inside the floating ark. They were all that was left in the world.

Noah and his family felt frightened and lost. The animals were restless, and they were all very tired of traveling. They looked out the window. There was nothing but water, miles and miles of water. They knew that God would take care of them, though, because God had made a promise to Noah.

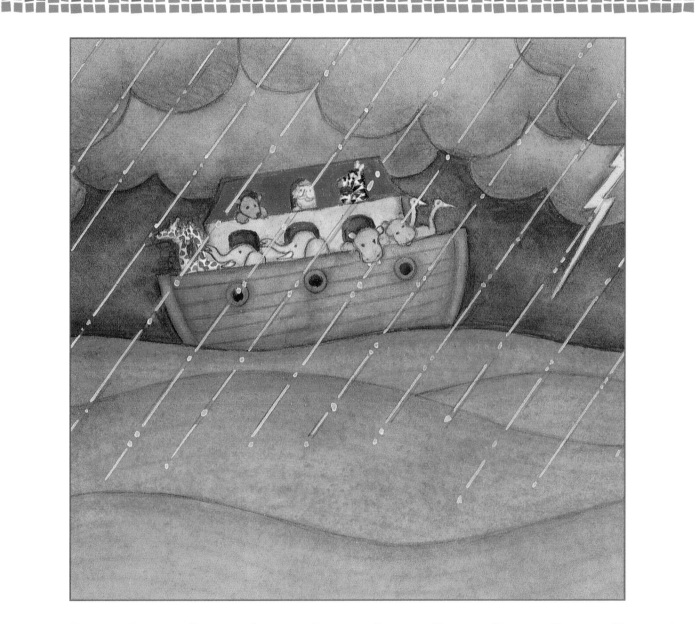

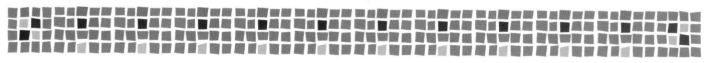

Finally, the rain stopped. Noah looked out the window. All he saw was a sea of water. It was not safe to leave the ark.

Over the next two weeks, the water sank lower and lower. The ark ground to a halt near the tops of the mountains of Ararat. Noah and his family were very happy to reach firm land, but they still did not know if there was enough dry land to settle on.

Noah and his wife decided to release a dove into the air. The dove flew away and returned before dark. There was still too much water. After seven days, Noah gently released the dove again. This time the bird came back with an olive branch. Noah was very pleased to see something green and growing. Noah waited patiently seven more days and then sent the dove once more. This time the dove did not return. Noah knew that there was enough dry land for them to safely leave the ark.

Then God spoke to Noah. "Go out of the ark and be free. The flood is over."

Two by two, the animals left the ark. They went out in search of homes where they could create new families.

Noah had trusted God. God was so pleased, he decided to make a special promise to Noah. He promised him that he would never bring another great flood.

To mark his promise, God created a beautiful rainbow of colors. He told Noah, "I have set my rainbow in the sky. The rainbow will be the sign of my promise to you and the earth. After each rain, look for the rainbow. It is my everlasting promise to you."

JOSEPH'S COAT

Adapted by Brian Conway

Illustrated by Jon Goodell

Joseph was a kind boy who lived with his family in the land of Canaan. He had ten older brothers and one younger brother. Their father was an old shepherd named Jacob. Jacob loved all of his sons, but he thought Joseph was the most caring of them all.

One day, Jacob surprised Joseph with a special gift. It was a brightly colored coat. The other sons were angry with their father. Jacob had never treated one son better than another, until he gave Joseph the coat. That made them angry at Joseph, too.

The brothers were also upset that they worked in the fields all day, while Joseph stayed home with Jacob. One morning, Jacob told Joseph, "You are old enough to work in the fields now. Go help your brothers."

Joseph worked very hard tending the sheep, but his brothers were not nice to him. They said many cruel things about Joseph and Jacob. At the end of the day, Joseph told Jacob what his brothers had said. Jacob punished his older sons, but this only made them more angry with Joseph.

That night and the next, Joseph had two strange dreams. In the first dream, Joseph worked in the fields with his brothers. Each brother had a stalk of wheat tied into a bundle. Joseph's bundle stood up on its own, but his brothers' bundles bowed down to Joseph's. When Joseph told his brothers about the dream, they got angry.

"We will never bow down to you!" they shouted.

In the next dream, the sun, the moon, and eleven stars bowed down to Joseph. He asked his father what it meant. Jacob thought the dreams could be God's way of speaking to this special boy, but he did not tell this to Joseph. Instead he said, "The stars must be your brothers, and the sun and the moon must be your parents."

To make up with his brothers, Joseph packed a basket of food and carried it out to the pasture. When Joseph's brothers saw him in the distance, they shouted, "Here comes the boy dreamer, the one who thinks he will rule over all of us! Let's get rid of him for good. That will teach our father to play favorites!"

The brothers made a plan to kill Joseph when he arrived. The oldest and wisest brother, Reuben, did not like that idea. "Let's just give him a good scare," he suggested.

Soon Joseph arrived with the treat for his brothers. They tore off his jacket and threw him into a pit. While Joseph cried for help, his brothers sat down to eat.

Just then, a caravan of traders rode by. Joseph's mean brothers sold Joseph as a slave to the traders. Before they went home, Joseph's brothers wiped animal blood on Joseph's coat and told their sad father that a wild animal must have killed their brother.

The traders sold Joseph to Egyptians. Although he was away from his family, Joseph was not alone. God was always with him. God had given Joseph the ability to understand the meanings of dreams.

After many years, word of Joseph's gift reached Pharaoh. Pharaoh had been having strange dreams and called on Joseph for help.

"These dreams tell the future of Egypt," Joseph said. "You will have seven good years. Food will be plentiful. But seven bad years will follow. The ground will dry up, and your people will be hungry."

"What can I do?" Pharaoh sighed.

"Find a wise man and put him in charge of saving food while there is plenty of it," Joseph said. "Then the people will not go hungry later."

Pharaoh liked Joseph's plan. He asked Joseph to be in charge of it. When the time of hunger came, Joseph's plan worked, and nobody in Egypt went hungry.

The people in other lands were not so lucky, though. In Canaan, Jacob and his family ran out of food. Joseph's brothers traveled to Egypt to buy food from the Pharaoh. They were taken to Joseph, but they did not recognize him. Joseph knew his brothers right away, but he waited. Joseph's brothers bowed down and pleaded for food. Joseph agreed to give them some. Then he invited his brothers to his home for lunch.

For lunch, Joseph made his brothers' favorite foods, just as he had done on the day he last saw them.

"It is I, your brother Joseph," he said. "God has brought you here to me. I love you, and I forgive you."

Joseph's brothers were amazed. Joseph invited them and the rest of their family to live with him in Egypt. The grateful brothers returned to Canaan, gathered their families, and went back to Egypt to be with Joseph. Jacob and Joseph were finally together again.

MIRIAM AND MOSES

Adapted by Sarah Toast

Illustrated by Kathy Mitchell

Jochebed worked long and hard in the fields. She was expecting a baby, and her husband, Amram, was forced to work far from their home. When Jochebed returned home from her long day, her children, Miriam and Aaron, ran to greet her.

"Sit and relax," Miriam told her mother, handing her a glass of sweetened water. After her mother finished her refreshing drink, Miriam asked her why she looked so troubled.

"I have dreadful news," said Jochebed. "It is not enough that Pharaoh has turned us into slaves and made our days a misery. Now Pharaoh is very afraid of us — afraid that we will rise up against him. He is more angry with our people and will surely treat us badly."

"Pharaoh already treats us badly," said Miriam.

"There is worse to come, my child," her mother said. "I heard in the fields today that Pharaoh has ordered the Israelite nurses to kill all little baby boys born to us, sparing only the baby girls."

"That is dreadful, Mother!" cried Miriam. "What if our new baby is a boy? What will we do?"

"Pray that God will help us," Jochebed said.

As the weeks passed, Jochebed became too weak to work in the fields any longer. Early each morning Miriam gathered reeds for her mother. Jochebed would weave the reeds into beautiful baskets that Miriam sold at the market.

After bringing the reeds home, Miriam went to the well where the women of Goshen drew water for their households and discussed the latest news.

One day a kind woman helped Miriam pour water from the well. "It is true," the woman whispered. "The Pharaoh has ordered all Egyptians to throw every Israelite baby boy into the Nile river."

Miriam ran home to tell her mother.

By the time Miriam got back to the house, the nurse had already been called. Jochebed had given birth to a beautiful son.

"Come here, children, and meet your new baby brother," said Jochebed proudly. "We must be very quiet. We cannot tell anyone besides our neighbors, and we must hide him from sight."

For three long months the family took care of the little baby boy without the Egyptians knowing about him. Jochebed continued to weave baskets at home. Miriam helped out with the chores. When Egyptians searched Israelite homes and yards, Jochebed hid her little baby in a basket.

Early one morning when Miriam was in the tall reeds at the river's edge, she heard people approaching. She saw the Pharaoh's beautiful daughter coming down to the river with her servants. "I have seen the Pharaoh's daughter here before," Miriam thought. "She may be the daughter of the Pharaoh, but she seems very pleasant. I must remember what days she comes here."

One morning Jochebed could not hide her worry from her daughter. "Sit down, child, I need to speak with you." Jochebed said. "The baby is now three months old. His cries are too loud to hide any longer. And he needs to be outdoors sometimes. I do not know how much longer we can possibly hide him."

"Do not worry," Miriam said. "I have a plan to save the baby."

Miriam and her mother made a special basket in the shape of a little boat. Before full light, Miriam and her mother quietly took the baby in the basket to the place on the riverbank where the Pharaoh's daughter came to bathe. There the Israelite mother and daughter set the basket in the thick reeds, where it would not drift downstream with the current. The basket bobbed gently on the water, lulling the baby to sleep.

Jochebed went back home to wait and pray. Miriam stayed hidden in the tall reeds and grasses. She waited until the Pharaoh's daughter came and spotted the baby in the little boat.

The Pharaoh's daughter picked up the baby. She knew he was in danger. "How can we take care of this child?" she asked aloud. "How shall we keep this baby safe?"

Miriam quietly stepped out from of the reeds and asked, "Shall I find an Israelite woman to nurse and take care of the baby for you?"

"If you can bring such a woman to me," Pharaoh's daughter said. "I will pay her to care for this child until he is old enough to leave her. I will name him Moses and someday he will be the Prince of Egypt!"

And that is how Miriam saved her brother, Moses.

MOSES AND PHARAOH

Adapted by Brian Conway

Illustrated by Kathy Mitchell

One day, an old man named Shaul said to his grandson Simeon, "It is time you learned the story of our people. I want to tell you about a tragic time for the Israelites, the time we spent in Egypt, and a great man named Moses who saved us from slavery.

"I was only a boy then, just about your age," Shaul started. "All of the Israelites were slaves to the terrible Pharaoh, ruler of Egypt. Everyone, even the children, worked all day and into the night, making bricks to build Pharaoh's city.

"One day I saw Moses walking proudly to Pharaoh's palace," said Shaul. "I was such a curious boy then. I dropped my work and crept away. I wanted to hear what this brave man had to say.

" 'Let God's people go!' Moses told Pharaoh. 'Set them free, or God will surely punish you.'

"Moses stood firmly before Pharaoh and his guards," Shaul said. "But Pharaoh did nothing. He got up and walked into the palace."

Shaul continued his story. "Days later I woke up to hear a strange rumbling throughout the city. When I listened more closely, it sounded like croaking. I looked outside and saw the land was covered with frogs! They were in the river, over the roads, on the rooftops, in the wells, and all over Pharaoh's palace! It was an amazing sight!"

"Where did they come from?" Simeon asked his grandfather.

"Moses had warned Pharaoh that many terrible plagues would fall over Egypt if God's people were not set free," Shaul explained. "This was one of those plagues. It was not the first sign that God sent to Egypt, and it would not be the last. Pharaoh promised to set the Israelites free, if only Moses would ask God to take the frogs away. But when the frogs were gone, Pharaoh broke his promise.

"God sent swarms of flies upon Egypt, he made the Egyptians' cattle sick, he pounded the land with hailstorms, and he took away the sunshine. Each time these tragedies fell on Egypt, Moses went to Pharaoh and demanded, 'Let God's people go!' "

"At last God's powers became too much for Pharaoh and his people," Shaul told his grandson. "He agreed to let us leave Egypt. Moses came to bring my family the good news.

" 'We must leave now,' he said, 'as quickly as we can.'

"We left Egypt with nothing and journeyed into the desert," Shaul said. "It was hot and dry, but at least we were free from Pharaoh and his soldiers. Then one day we saw an army of Egyptians coming after us. Pharaoh had changed his mind again. Pharaoh wanted to bring us back to Egypt. But Moses was our leader, and God was our savior.

"I saw a miracle that day," Shaul added. "With the Pharaoh and his men chasing us, we came upon a sea. We had nowhere to turn. Then Moses raised his hand over the sea, and the waters divided.

"Once we had crossed, Moses turned back toward the sea and raised his hand again. The water flowed over Pharaoh and his soldiers."

"We were safe," said Shaul, "and we continued our difficult journey through the desert."

"What happened? How did you survive?" asked Simeon.

"It is not a happy story, but I will tell you now," said Shaul. "We walked through the hot desert with very little to eat for many months. We suffered greatly, but still we sang to God and prayed, and he provided food for us.

"Then one day Moses told everyone to wait for him, and he climbed up to a mountaintop. He said he was going to talk to God. He was gone for a long time. Some of the Israelites did not want to wait. Finally Moses returned with two tablets containing the laws that God had spoken to him. They were Ten Commandments from God, and we still follow them today."

"I know them all, Grandfather," said Simeon proudly. "You taught them to me."

"We followed the laws that God had commanded," Shaul continued. "And we followed Moses as he led us through the desert. God took care of us. He brought us to this place, which we call Israel. It is our promised land, our country, and our home.

"God watched over his children in the desert," said Shaul. "He watches over us wherever we are. Once we had a great hero, Moses, to remind us of that. Now we have each other. We have the Ten Commandments to guide us, and we have a very important story to tell our children and our grandchildren."

WALLS OF JERICHO

Adapted by Lisa Harkrader

Illustrated by Max Kolding

A boy named Peter walked beside the River Jordan with his father. They saw a pile of big round stones. Peter asked, "What's that?"

"These are the twelve stones, one for each of the twelve tribes of Israel," said his father. "These stones remind us of the miracle."

"What miracle?" Peter asked, looking out across the wide river.

"Ah, you were too young to remember," his father said. "You see, the Israelites had escaped from Egypt. Moses had died, and Joshua was now leading the Israelites to the Promised Land. When they got to the River Jordan, it was swollen to the top of its banks. The Israelite priests were carrying the Ark of the Covenant, the chest that held the Ten Commandments. God told Joshua to send the priests into the river."

"Into the river?" asked Peter. "Are you sure that is what God told Joshua? It does not seem right. They would all drown!"

"But they did not," said his father. "And that was the first miracle."

Peter's father continued, "When the priests stepped into the river it stopped flowing. The priests stood there while the Israelites crossed the dry riverbed. When everyone had reached the other side, and the priests stepped onto the bank, the river began flowing again. But that was not the only miracle. Do you want to hear what happened next?"

"Oh, yes!" said Peter. He settled down beside the pile of stones and listened as his father told the story.

"After the Israelites crossed the river, they had to pass through the city of Jericho to get to the Promised Land. A great stone wall surrounded the city. The only way in or out was through iron gates.

"The people of Jericho knew the River Jordan had stopped flowing when the Israelites crossed. They knew God was helping the Israelites, and they were afraid. The king of Jericho ordered the people to shut the iron gates. When Joshua and the Israelites got to Jericho, they found the gates locked. Joshua walked around the wall, looking for a way to get inside. But it was no use. There was no way in."

"Joshua headed toward the gates and came upon a man holding a sword. Joshua stopped and asked, 'Are you our friend or our enemy?'

" 'I am the commander of God's army,' said the man. 'Listen carefully to what I am about to tell you.'

"Joshua listened. This stranger was God's messenger. When the man finished speaking, Joshua knew what God wanted him to do. He ran back to camp and gathered the priests around him.

" 'Lift the Ark of the Covenant,' Joshua said, 'and carry it around the city. Seven of you will walk in front of the Ark, blowing horns.'

"The priests set off around the wall, blowing their horns, while the Israelites followed quietly behind. They circled the city once, then went back to their camp. The next morning, the Israelites rose at dawn. Again the priests carried the Ark around Jericho. Again seven priests trumpeted their horns. And again the Israelites followed quietly. They circled the city once, then went back to their camp."

"The Isrealites did this for six days. On the seventh day, Joshua said, 'The priests will carry the Ark of the Covenant and blow their horns, just as before. And we will follow quietly, just as before. But today we will circle the city seven times. On the seventh time, listen closely. I will tell you what to do.'

"The Israelites marched around the city six times. On the seventh time, Joshua yelled, 'Shout! Cheer! God has given you the city!'

"The priests trumpeted their horns. The Israelites shouted as loudly as they could. Above the shouting they could hear cracks and groans. The cracks spread across the walls. The walls of Jericho began to tremble.

"The Israelites shouted louder and louder. One stone fell from the wall, then another and another. The walls of Jericho tumbled to the ground in a pile of dust. It was truly a miracle! The Israelites cheered. They were able to pass through the city."

"And that," said Peter's father, "is how the Israelites conquered the great stone walls of Jericho. That is how they passed through Jericho on their way to the Promised Land."

"They did not use swords?" asked Peter. "Or spears?"

"No," Peter's father said, shaking his head. "They had a tool more powerful than a thousand swords and spears. They had the most powerful tool of all — they had their faith in God."

RUTH AND NAOMI

Adapted by Leslie Lindecker

Illustrated by Marty Noble

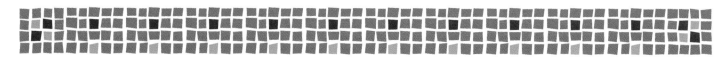

Naomi was a woman who had lived for many years in a far-away country called Moab. She had traveled there with her husband and two sons. They made a happy life together.

As her sons grew up, they married two young women from Moab. Their names were Orpah and Ruth. Naomi welcomed Orpah and Ruth into her home, loving them as if they were her own daughters.

One day Naomi's husband became ill and eventually he passed away. Naomi's sons also got sick and died. This left Naomi, Orpah, and Ruth alone and very sad.

Without her husband at her side, Naomi became homesick for the town where she grew up. Ruth tried to comfort her, but Naomi decided to return to her home in Bethlehem. Naomi had been gone a long time. The thought of returning home brought Naomi great comfort.

"I love both of you," Naomi told her two daughters-in-law, "but I miss my family in Bethlehem. I would like to return there to live."

Once the young women helped pack up the household, Naomi was ready to travel. "The two of you should return to your families here in Moab," Naomi said. "You are both young enough to marry again and have children. I am older and will not get married again. Although I will miss you both, it is best that I go alone."

Orpah cried at the thought of leaving Naomi. She kissed Naomi on the cheek, gave her a hug, and said, "I will miss you. You have been very kind to me. Have a safe journey to Bethlehem." Orpah picked up her bundle and went back to her family's home.

The thought of leaving Naomi made Ruth very sad. "Please do not ask me to leave you," Ruth said. "Where you go, I will go. Where you sleep, I will sleep. Your family is my family, and your God is my God."

Naomi was pleased that Ruth wanted to stay with her. The two women picked up their bundles and began their walk to Bethlehem. It would be a very long trip. Naomi and Ruth prayed together that God would provide for them on their journey.

Ruth and Naomi walked for many days to reach Bethlehem. They arrived at the city as the grain harvest began. Ruth set her bundle down. She turned to Naomi and said, "Let me go into these fields. I can gather the grain dropped by the people who work there. We will have grain to pound into flour. I can bake bread for us to eat."

Naomi rested as Ruth went into the field nearby. Ruth walked behind the reapers, gathering the grain they dropped as they worked. Ruth worked all day.

Late in the afternoon, a man named Boaz came to the field to see how well the harvest was going. Boaz was in charge of the workers. He noticed the pretty young woman following his workers. Boaz called over one of the reapers. "Who is that woman in the field?" he asked.

"She is from Moab. Her name is Ruth," the worker replied. "She traveled here with Naomi and asked if she could gather the grain we drop so they would have something to eat. Since she has been such a great help to Naomi, we did not think that you would mind."

And Boaz did not mind. In fact, he was pleased to help this woman and Naomi. Boaz went and introduced himself to Ruth.

"I have heard good things about you," said Boaz. "You take care of your mother-in-law. You are kind to others and help my workers. Please continue to work in my fields. My workers will not bother you. When you are thirsty, please drink from my water pots. When I bring food for my workers, I want you to eat with them."

"May God bless you and your family," Ruth said. When Boaz brought food for his workers, Ruth ate with them. She saved part of her food and took it to Naomi.

Naomi was pleased with the food and the grain. "Who was this man who gave you food and grain?" Naomi asked. Ruth told Naomi about meeting Boaz and what he had said to her.

"Boaz is the brother of my husband," Naomi said. "He is a good and kind man. May God bless him for his kindness toward us."

Boaz continued to watch Ruth as she worked in his fields each day. He talked with her and saw how much Ruth loved Naomi. Boaz became very fond of Ruth.

Boaz was a man of strong faith. He went to Ruth one day and said, "I would like for you to become my wife. Your mother-in-law, Naomi, may live with us, and I will take care of you both."

Ruth and Boaz were soon married, and Naomi lived with them in their home. Ruth had a baby boy. They named the baby Obed, and they all thanked God for their blessings of home and family.

SAMUEL

Adapted by Brian Conway

Illustrated by Carolyn Croll

Samuel lived with Eli, the old priest at the temple. Eli was good to Samuel, but one night Samuel asked, "Why do I live here? Why don't I live with my parents?"

"Your mother will come soon," Eli said. "You can ask her then."

Samuel's parents came every week to see their son. Sometimes Samuel's father was unable to make the trip, but Samuel's mother Hannah had never missed a visit. On her next visit, Samuel asked her why he lived with Eli. As Hannah tucked him into bed, she told him how he came to live in the temple. She had waited many years to tell Samuel this story. Now he was old enough to understand.

"For a long time," she began, "your father and I had no children. We wanted a child more than anything in the world. We prayed each day that God would give us a child. Many years passed. One day, I was very sad. I thought perhaps God had not heard our prayers, and I wondered what I could do to please him. I came to this temple and prayed here all day."

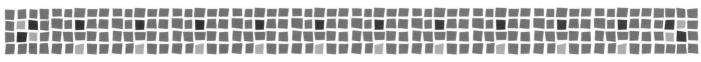

"I promised God that if he gave me a son, I would return my son to him. I was so sad that I started crying. Eli heard me crying. He assured me that God had heard my prayers. Soon I found out I was going to have a baby. Your father and I were so happy!

"Finally, you arrived. You filled our house with such joy! We gave you lots of love and attention. I told our neighbors, 'This is Samuel. He is a gift from God.'

"I brought you here so you could learn to be God's special servant. God had given us a gift, and we knew we had to give that gift back to God, just as I had promised. We brought you here the day you grew too big for your cradle. Eli assured us he would teach you to be a priest. He said, 'I will treat Samuel as a gift from God.' "

Samuel cried, "I want to live with you and Father. I always have to study. Even Eli's sons get to play more than I do. I am inside all day, while they are outside enjoying themselves. They watch me through the window and laugh because I am always reading. Let me go home."

"When we serve God, sometimes we have to give up things that are important to us," said Hannah. "You are a very special boy, and you must study very hard to be prepared to learn how to serve God."

That night Samuel prayed. "Thank you, God, for all my blessings. I promise I'll work hard to be your special gift. I really do not understand why I live here, and I miss my parents, but I will study hard for you."

Samuel fell asleep. He woke when he heard someone call his name. He looked around to see who was calling him. He even checked under his bed. He went to Eli's room and asked, "Did you call me, Eli?"

"No," Eli yawned. "You must be dreaming. Please go back to bed."

Samuel climbed back into bed. Again he heard a voice calling him, and again he went to Eli. As before, Eli said, "I did not call you."

Samuel heard the voice a third time. "Eli," Samuel said, "Someone is calling me. I even checked under my bed. It is not a dream."

Eli saw the serious look on Samuel's face. Eli said, "What did the voice say to you?"

"It said my name three times," Samuel said.

Eli thought maybe God was calling for Samuel. "If you hear the voice again," said Eli, "answer, 'God, your servant is listening.' "

Samuel did as Eli told him. When he heard his name again, Samuel said, "God, your servant is listening."

God appeared to Samuel and told Samuel his plan. "When you grow up, you will take Eli's place as the priest of this temple. And you will serve me as a prophet. Work hard and study the scripture. Listen to Eli and to your parents. These things will make you a good priest. Above all, you must keep the promise you made in your prayer. Be a special gift to me, as I am to you."

"I will, God," said Samuel. "I promise."

Samuel was so excited, he could not sleep. This was the most important day in his life. His mother had taught him that he was a gift from God, and God had given him a gift — the gift of his word.

In the morning, Samuel told Eli what God had said. Eli was not at all surprised. He knew all along that Samuel was a special boy. Later, Samuel and Eli walked to Samuel's parents' house. Samuel could not wait to tell his parents a story. It was the story of a very special visit. It was the story of Samuel's gift from God.

DAVID AND GOLIATH

Adapted by Catherine McCafferty

Illustrated by Anthony Lewis

David was the youngest of eight sons. He felt like nobody noticed him, even though he was a good shepherd and a skilled harp player. Then one day God sent the prophet Samuel to David's house to name the next king of Israel. David had seven older brothers, but Samuel announced that God had chosen David!

David was excited. He was ready to go to the palace right away. He was disappointed when Samuel told him to stay and continue tending the sheep for his father.

Soon David's three oldest brothers left to join the army. Saul, who was Israel's present king, needed help protecting Israel from the Philistines. David wished he could go with his brothers.

One morning, as David was watching the sheep, a lion ran off with a small lamb. David chased the lion. He aimed a stone at the lion with his sling and hit the beast in the head! The lion dropped the lamb and ran away. "Even though nobody saw me fight the lion," David said, "one day I will prove that I can be a brave soldier and a strong king."

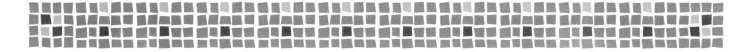

David's chance to prove himself came, but not as he expected. One of King Saul's servants fetched David. The king was very worried about the war and needed some music to soothe him. The king heard that David played the harp very well. David's father agreed to let his son play for the king in the evening if the boy would tend the sheep during the day. David played for the king every night until the king fell asleep. The king grew fond of David. His music made the king feel better.

When David's brothers had been at war for forty days, their father sent David to the battlefront with some food. The soldiers were shouting and running toward the enemy. David left the food with a guard and hurried to the soldiers. Suddenly the soldiers stopped.

Goliath, the Philistines' leader, had stepped onto the battlefield. He was almost ten feet tall! His bronze armor alone looked as if it weighed more than David. And the spear Goliath carried looked mighty enough to stab the sky. "Choose one man to fight against me," roared Goliath. "If he kills me, the Philistines will be your slaves. But if I kill him, you shall become our slaves."

The Israelites ran away. David realized this was his chance to prove himself. He went to the king and said, "I will fight Goliath."

"You cannot fight the Philistine alone," Saul said kindly but firmly. "You are only a boy. Goliath has been a warrior all his life."

David described his battle with the lion. "I will defeat Goliath just as I conquered the lion," David said. "God will protect me."

"Go, and may God be with you!" Saul declared.

The king ordered his servant to bring a suit of armor, and David tried it on. It was so heavy that David could hardly move. Saul gave David a large sword. David grasped the handle but could barely lift the heavy blade. Bravely, he smiled up at Saul. He was ready to defend Israel now. But not with the armor, and not with the sword.

As respectfully as he could, David told the king, "I cannot walk in this armor. I am not used to it."

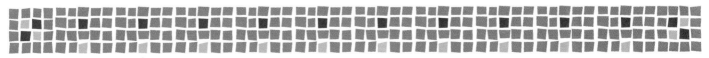

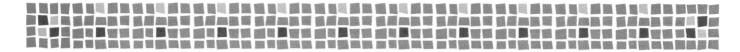

With the king's permission, he took off the armor. Then David went to a nearby stream and gathered five stones. He pulled out his sling and tightened his grip around it. He was ready to face Goliath. David returned to the battlefront. With his brothers, the king, and the rest of the army behind him, David walked toward Goliath.

The giant looked down at David and laughed. He told the Israelites to send one man, and they sent a boy!

Goliath took a step forward. David did not move. Instead, he said, "You come against me with a mighty spear and heavy armor, but I come against you in the name of God. This same God, whose armies you have dared to insult, will deliver you into my hands."

David reached into his pouch for a stone. As Goliath's shadow fell over him, David loaded the sling and whirled the rock in a circle, faster and faster. Goliath let out a fierce war cry and raised his spear. David took aim and let the stone fly. Whooosh! Thud! The stone met its mark.

As the stone hit his forehead, Goliath dropped his spear and crashed to the ground. David had beaten Goliath! The Israelites cheered and drove the Philistines far from Israel. David's brothers lifted him onto their shoulders. The other soldiers danced and shouted.

Saul stepped onto the battlefield. "From this day forward," he said to David, "you shall be the commander of my army!"

David bowed to Saul, accepting his new position. Then he took Goliath's armor and spear. David wanted them as reminders of God's power. With God beside him, David did not have to be big to be brave.

ELIJAH AND ELISHA

Adapted by Elizabeth Olson

Illustrated by Lyn Martin

King Ahab was a bad king who worshiped false gods. Elijah the prophet did God's work and served the Lord well. One day, God punished Ahab by sending a drought to Ahab's kingdom.

Elijah delivered the news to the king. "King Ahab, because you do not listen to the word of God, no rain will fall in your kingdom for many years," said Elijah. "You will not even see a drop of dew."

God loved Elijah and wanted to protect him. "Elijah, you must leave the kingdom of Ahab," said God. "I will show you a safe place where you can live for many years."

God led Elijah to a lovely brook in the hills. "Here you will be safe," said God. "You can drink from this clear stream. Every day, a raven will bring you bread and meat in the morning and evening."

For several years, Elijah lived in the beautiful place in the hills. The friendly raven made sure that Elijah always had enough to eat. Elijah gave thanks to God for his blessings.

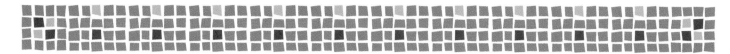

One day, the stream stopped running and the ravens did not appear. God said, "Elijah, you are a faithful servant. Now you must go to Sidon. A kind woman there will take care of you."

Elijah obeyed God. For several days he walked through the desert to Sidon. At the city gate, he met the woman. He told her, "I am very hungry and thirsty from my journey. Could you please bring me a drink of water and a small piece of bread?"

"I would gladly give you what I have," she said, "but I have barely enough flour and oil to make bread for my son."

"God will not let you go hungry," said Elijah. "Please make a small loaf of bread for me from what you have. Then make a loaf for your son and another for yourself. Your oil and flour will never run out."

The woman followed Elijah's instructions. When she finished making the third loaf of bread, she was amazed to see the jar of flour and jug of oil overflow onto her table.

Elijah the prophet continued to serve God for many years. One day, God sent him to Damascus.

"You are getting older, Elijah," said God. "The time has come for you to have a helper. Go to the fields, where you will find a young farmer named Elisha."

Elijah obeyed God. He soon found Elisha plowing a field. Elijah put his coat over the young man's shoulders. Elisha understood the will of God. He put down the plow, said goodbye to his parents, and went with Elijah. Together the two men walked through the fields.

"God always protects those who follow him," said Elijah.

When the two men came upon the River Jordan, Elijah touched the blessed coat to the river. Elisha could not believe his eyes as the water divided to create a dry path. Elijah motioned for Elisha to follow him along the path. As Elisha followed, he said, "Elijah, I want to be just like you. I will serve God and follow him."

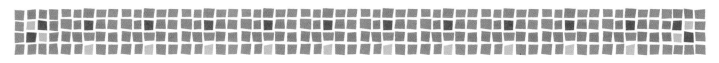

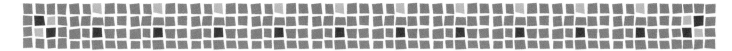

When the day came for Elijah to go to heaven, Elisha was very sad.

Elijah placed his hands on the young man's shoulders and said, "Do not worry, Elisha. God will protect you and comfort you when I am gone. Plus, I promise to leave you something very important." These words made Elisha feel better.

Suddenly, a beautiful chariot pulled by magnificent horses appeared in the sky. The horses swooped down to the ground and stopped in front of Elijah, who understood the will of God.

"I must go to heaven now," said Elijah. "Goodbye, Elisha."

The older man climbed into the chariot, which immediately began to rise back into the clouds.

"I will miss you!" called Elisha, waving. Just then, he noticed that Elijah had dropped his wonderful coat on the ground. This was the very important gift Elijah had mentioned.

Elisha missed his friend, but he continued to serve God and help others. Elisha became the priest at the shrine where the covenant chest was kept.

One day a woman came to the shrine crying. Elisha asked her what was wrong. "We have everything we need," the woman told Elijah. "But we have always wanted a son."

Elisha prayed to God to bring the couple a child. God answered his prayers. Elisha told the woman she would have a son in a year. One year later, the woman had a baby boy.

ESTHER

Adapted by Lisa Harkrader

Illustrated by Loretta Lustig

Esther stood before King Xerxes. She had never been inside the royal hall before. She had never seen so much gold and marble and silk, so many finely dressed noblemen, or so many servants. She had never seen the king up close. He had called her, and now he sat on his throne watching her. She tried not to let him see her tremble.

Her cousin, Mordecai, waited behind her. Esther's parents had died when she was very young, and Mordecai had raised her. He was the only father she had ever known.

"Esther, you are the most beautiful woman in the land," the king said. "You are also kind and intelligent. I want you to be my wife."

Esther gasped. Mordecai smiled. The king placed a crown on Esther's head.

The king gathered all of his officers. "I invite you all to a banquet," he said. "We will feast on roasted meats, desserts, and fine wine. We will celebrate our new queen — Queen Esther."

King Xerxes' most trusted advisor was a man named Haman. Haman demanded that people bow down as he walked by. One day, not long after Esther had become queen, Haman passed through the palace gates. Everyone bowed except for Esther's cousin, Mordecai.

"I order you to bow like all these other peasants," said Haman, glaring at Mordecai.

"I bow only before God," said Mordecai. "I bow because I worship him. I respect you, Haman, but I do not worship you."

This made Haman angry. At the next royal council meeting, Haman announced that a dangerous group of people in the kingdom refused to obey the king's laws. The king did not know that Haman was talking about Mordecai and his family. He issued an order that these disloyal people should be killed.

When Mordecai heard the order, he shook with fear. He could not let Haman kill his family. He raced to the palace to find Esther.

"You must beg the king to spare us," Mordecai told Esther.

"But you know the king's rule," said Esther. "He does not like anyone, not even me, to speak to him without an invitation. If he does not hold out his golden scepter to show he approves, the uninvited visitor can be thrown into prison. If I speak to him and he gets angry, it will make things worse. I will wait for an invitation to the royal hall."

"Do not wait too long," said Mordecai. "We have only a few days."

Esther waited. One day passed, then another. On the third day, she could wait no longer. She put on her finest robes and hurried to the hall. Once more she found herself trembling before the king.

"My king," said Esther, her voice shaking. "You did not invite me here, but I must speak to you. It is important."

Esther waited. She watched the king's face. He smiled and held out his scepter. Esther nearly collapsed in relief.

Esther knew that the king would be angry if she asked him to change his royal order. Luckily, she also knew that he never turned down a delicious meal.

"I have prepared a banquet," said Esther. "I would like for you and Haman to dine with me."

That night they ate all of the king's favorite foods. The king was pleased. Esther wanted to be sure she had won his favor, so she invited the king and Haman to dine with her again the next night. The king and Haman feasted once more on the food Esther had prepared.

"This was the most delicious meal I have ever eaten," the king told Esther. "If you wanted half the kingdom, I would give it to you now."

Esther took a deep breath and said, "I do not want your kingdom. I only want to save my family."

The king frowned. "Your family? I do not understand."

"Yes," said Esther. "Soon, they will be killed. It is a royal order,"

King Xerxes turned to Haman. "These are the people you said were a threat to me? Esther's people? You tricked me!"

"No!" cried Haman. "I did not trick you. I tried to protect you. Surely you believe me. I am your most trusted advisor!"

"Not any longer," said the king. He banished Haman from the kingdom, so he could never harm Esther or her people.

DANIEL

Adapted by Lora Kalkman

Illustrated by Nancy Woodman

In the kingdom of Babylon lived a man named Daniel. Besides being a hard worker, he was a true servant of God. God had blessed him with wisdom and intelligence, and Daniel was grateful. He pledged always to serve God.

One day, King Darius asked Daniel to come to his castle. The king said, "Daniel, you are a good man. You are intelligent and loyal. I would like you to become second in command of the entire kingdom. If anything should ever happen to me, you shall be in charge."

Daniel was honored. He accepted the king's offer graciously.

"I know you can be trusted to make good decisions and to do what is right," said King Darius. "The people of Babylon will surely benefit from your wisdom."

"Thank you," Daniel replied. "I promise to be devoted and loyal. I shall always serve you to the best of my ability, and I will do what is right for the people of Babylon."

King Darius was very pleased with Daniel. The king gave him more and more responsibilities, because he knew Daniel could be trusted to make wise and just decisions. Daniel was happy in his work. He prayed three times a day, thanking God for his many blessings.

Unlike Daniel, some of the king's advisors were not very good men. They did not work hard and they spent much of their time complaining about Daniel. They thought King Darius gave Daniel too much power. They came up with a plan to catch Daniel making a mistake. That proved very difficult. Daniel did not make many mistakes. This upset them even more.

"What can we do to get Daniel in trouble?" the jealous advisors asked each other one evening.

"I have often seen Daniel praying to God," said one man. "We will urge the king to issue a formal decree. The decree will command that any person caught praying to anyone besides the king shall be thrown into the lions' den."

The advisors met with King Darius. After the jealous advisors had told him their idea, the king was not sure what to do. He wished he could consult with Daniel, but Daniel was working elsewhere in the kingdom. Finally, the king grew weary of listening to his advisors. He decided to issue the decree they requested.

"And you must make this command unchangeable," the jealous advisors urged. "No matter what happens, anyone caught praying to anyone besides you must be thrown into the lions' den."

"So be it," King Darius proclaimed.

When Daniel returned, he learned of the king's decree. Saddened by this news, Daniel went to his room to pray. He said to God, "The decree says I must not pray to you, but you shall always be first in my life. How can I be loyal to the king while serving you?"

The jealous advisors had followed Daniel, and saw him praying. They ran to tell the king that Daniel had disobeyed the decree.

King Darius was very upset. He realized that the advisors had tricked him. He tried desperately to think of a way to save Daniel from being thrown into the lions' den, but the wicked advisors reminded the king that he had no choice. Daniel had disobeyed the command, and it could not be changed.

With a heavy heart, King Darius summoned Daniel. He said, "Dear Daniel, I do not wish to do this, but I have no choice. I urge you to pray to your God. Perhaps he can save you from the hungry lions."

Soon after, the king's advisors led Daniel to a large, dark cave. Daniel bravely walked inside. He knew that God was watching over him. The king's guards covered the opening with a huge stone.

"Dear God," Daniel prayed, "I know that you are the greatest king of all. I will always honor you. I hope others will come to do the same."

All through the night, Daniel prayed to God. Amazingly, the lions did not harm Daniel.

The king could not eat or sleep all night. In the morning, he rushed to the lions' den and commanded his guards to roll away the stone. He called, "Daniel, has your God saved you from the lions?"

The king was overjoyed to hear Daniel reply, "Yes, King Darius, God has saved me. He is truly the mightiest king in all the world."

King Darius agreed. He immediately helped Daniel from the lions' den and punished the wicked advisors who had tricked him. Then the king issued a new decree: "From this day forward, all people shall pray to Daniel's God, for he is truly the greatest king of all."

JONAH AND THE WHALE

Adapted by Brian Conway

Illustrated by Laura Merer

Jonah was one of God's faithful servants. He lived a simple life in a quiet village. He prayed to God and followed all of God's commandments. One day, God chose Jonah for a special task. God wanted Jonah to take a journey to a nearby city. This city, called Nineveh, had turned to sin and violence.

"The people in Nineveh have forgotten me," God said. "Go to that city, Jonah, and bring the people my word."

Jonah had heard many frightful stories about the city of Nineveh. It was a terrible place. People were sinful there. They were often mean to each other, and they were always mean to strangers.

Jonah was afraid. He did not want to go to Nineveh. He thought the people would not listen to him. He thought the wicked people of Nineveh might want to hurt him.

In his fear, Jonah thought only of saving himself. He did not think of God's wishes. Jonah ran away from Nineveh. He ran away from God.

Jonah went away to a city by the sea. He wanted to leave his country. Jonah thought he could hide from God in a faraway place. At the port, he found a boat that was about to leave for a distant land. Jonah paid his fare and climbed aboard the boat.

"Where are you traveling to?" said one friendly passenger.

"I do not know," answered Jonah sadly. "I only know that I am going away from here."

As the ship sailed away from the shore, Jonah went down below the deck. There, he fell asleep. He slept peacefully for a while, but he awoke with a start. A great storm had risen from the sea. The boat was tossing back and forth among the wild waves.

"What is happening?" Jonah asked a passenger.

"A terrible storm came upon us suddenly," the passenger replied. "We had no warning. We are in serious danger, I'm afraid."

The passengers huddled together inside the boat. They prayed to many different gods to save them. Jonah saw the fear in their faces, but he did not pray. He knew that God had sent this storm, and he knew he was a fool to think he could hide from God.

Jonah stood up and said, "The storm is meant for me. I ran away from God, and only I should face the consequences. Throw me into the waves, and you will be saved."

"But you will die!" the men said. "We cannot do that."

"Trust me," Jonah said bravely. "It is the only way,"

The men did as Jonah asked. As soon as he disappeared beneath the waves, the storm stopped. As he sank into the sea, Jonah prayed.

A giant whale came up from the depths of the sea. It swallowed Jonah in one swift gulp. Like the terrible storm, this giant whale was sent by God. Jonah understood.

Jonah sat inside the belly of the whale and waited. It was very dark and damp, but at least he was able to breathe again.

Jonah thought for a long time about what had happened. "I should have done as God asked," he whispered. "I was a fool."

Jonah was happy to be alive, but he was trapped inside the whale. He wondered if he would ever be free again. Jonah knew that he was not completely alone. God, he understood, was always with him. Jonah asked God to forgive him.

"I was afraid," Jonah prayed, "and I ran away from you. I will never run away from you again. I should have known that you would keep me safe. I should have known that you would never let danger come to me. And I know that now, God. I trust you more than ever."

Jonah spent three days and three nights inside the whale. He was not afraid. He had faith in God's goodness. In his prayers, Jonah promised to always serve God.

Finally, the whale opened its mouth and Jonah was free. He swam out of the whale to the shore, where God spoke to Jonah a second time. "Go now to Nineveh, and bring the people my message."

This time Jonah obeyed. He walked to Nineveh. At every city gate and in every marketplace, Jonah told his story.

He warned the people of Nineveh that they could not run away from God. The people listened. And since Jonah was spreading the message to God's people, he knew he had nothing to fear again.

THE BIRTH OF JESUS

Adapted by Suzanne Lieurance

Illustrated by Terri Steiger

A long time ago, there was a young woman named Mary. She had promised to marry a man named Joseph. One day, God sent the angel Gabriel to visit Mary. She was in the garden, gathering fruits and vegetables, when she saw Gabriel standing above her.

"Greetings," said Gabriel. "Do not be afraid, Mary. I have wonderful news for you. You have found favor with God. You will be with child and give birth to a son! You shall name the child Jesus."

Mary stared up at Gabriel. "How could this be?" she asked. "I am not even married yet."

Gabriel answered, "The Holy Spirit will visit you. The holy one to be born will be called the Son of God."

At first, Mary did not know what to say. "God has chosen me?" she whispered. "I am the Lord's servant. May it be as you have said."

The angel smiled and floated away.

Months passed, and Mary was nearly ready to deliver her baby. But first, she and Joseph had to go to Bethlehem so they could pay their taxes. Mary rode a donkey that Joseph led.

It was a long, hard ride, but Mary did not complain. Joseph guided the donkey over hills and through valleys for many, many days. Finally, just as the sun set one evening, they saw the lights of Bethlehem.

As the sky grew dark, Joseph started looking for a place to spend the night. He knocked on the doors of many inns, but all the rooms were taken. Many people had traveled to Bethlehem.

At the last inn Joseph could find, the innkeeper shook his head. "I am sorry," he said, "we have no room here."

"Please," Joseph said. "She could deliver her baby any minute."

The innkeeper scratched his head. "Well, I suppose you can stay in the stable with the animals. It is warm there."

Joseph took Mary and the donkey to the stable. This would be their room for the night. Joseph tried to make Mary comfortable. He cleared a space for her and made a bed out of soft hay so she could rest. They were very grateful.

That evening, Mary gave birth to her baby. Just as the angel Gabriel had told her to do, Mary named him Jesus. Mary and Joseph gazed at the tiny baby with joy.

Mary carefully wrapped the baby in strips of cloth. They did not have a cradle, so Joseph laid him to sleep in the manger. The baby fell asleep instantly.

While Joseph, Mary, and baby Jesus were sleeping, a shepherd boy and his father were tending their sheep in a nearby village. Just as any other night, the father and son guarded their flock and talked quietly to keep themselves awake.

"Look!" the boy said, pointing to the sky.

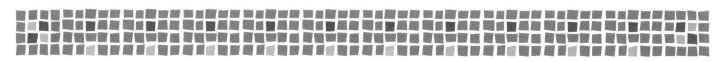

The father looked up. A beautiful, bright shining star had appeared. It beamed down like a spotlight.

As they gazed at the star, the sky suddenly filled with angels dressed in flowing robes.

The angels looked down at the shepherd boy and his father and smiled. Then one of the angels spoke to them.

"Do not be frightened," said the angel, "for we come with great news for you. The world shall rejoice tonight! On this day, in the city of Bethlehem, a Savior has been born to you. He is Christ the Lord. Go and see him. Go and witness the miracle. You will find a baby wrapped in cloths and lying in a manger. Follow the bright shining star. It will lead you to Bethlehem." The angels sang a hymn of praise, and then, as suddenly as they had come, they were gone.

The shepherd and his son looked at one another with amazement. "Come," the father whispered, "let's go."

In Bethlehem, the star was shining directly over the tiny stable. The shepherd boy quietly opened the door to the stable and walked in. There he found Mary and Joseph, and the baby. Just as the angels had said, the baby was wrapped in cloths and lying in a manger.

The shepherd boy knelt down before the baby to pray. As the boy prayed, other shepherds gathered behind him. They had all followed the bright star. They had all come from far away to meet little Jesus. They had all come to witness this beautiful miracle.

JESUS AT THE TEMPLE

Adapted by Megan Musgrave

Illustrated by Jerry Hartsten

Jesus grew up in a small town called Nazareth in the country of Galilee. His parents, Mary and Joseph, always knew that Jesus was a very special child. God had chosen Jesus to be the savior of all people. One day, people would call Jesus the Son of God. But when he was just a little boy, Jesus was a lot like other children.

One morning when Jesus was going out to play, Mary stopped him. "Jesus, I need your help this morning, remember?" she said. "We need to pack for our trip to Jerusalem for Passover. It is a long journey, so we all need to work together."

They strapped the bigger bags onto the donkey, but Jesus and Joseph carried the smaller bags so that Mary would have room to ride on the donkey. They set off for Jerusalem.

Jesus was a very curious child. He asked Mary and Joseph many questions. Jesus asked everyone questions! As they walked to Jerusalem, Jesus asked them to tell him the story of Passover again. Jesus knew the story by heart, but he still enjoyed hearing it again and again.

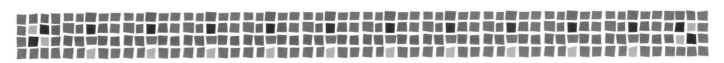

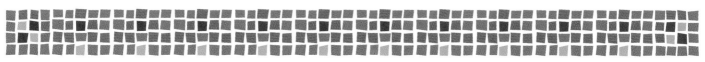

After journeying for many days, Jesus and his family reached Jerusalem, where many Jewish people had gathered to celebrate Passover. When it was time for the Passover dinner, the rabbi said a special blessing. Everyone at the table took a drink from a goblet of wine that was passed around and then washed their hands in preparation of the meal. Jesus' aunt began passing plates of unique food around the table.

"What is this, Father?" Jesus asked, holding up a sprig of green.

"That is karpas, Jesus," explained Joseph, taking some karpas for himself. "We dip parsley in salt water to remind us of the tears shed by our people when they were in slavery."

Jesus tasted the karpas. He tried all the different foods that were passed to him while the rabbi retold the story of Passover. Then the rabbi said some more special blessings before the rest of the meal was served. The family also told stories and recited psalms during dinner.

The next morning, Mary woke Jesus early. "We need to go visit the temple so that we can say prayers and thank God for bringing us here safely," Mary explained.

The temple was a large, beautiful building at the end of the street. It had a tall, arched doorway and smooth, sun-bleached walls.

"This is much bigger than our temple in Nazareth," said Jesus. Jesus and his parents joined the worship service there, and afterwards they visited with the elder rabbis of the temple.

"Jesus, you may come back and visit us anytime you like," the elders at the temple told him.

After visiting with his relatives for a few more days, Jesus began to get restless. "No one will mind if I go back to the temple again," he thought. "After all, the elders did invite me back for a visit." Jesus ran to the temple and found the elders gathered inside, talking. The elders enjoyed talking to Jesus very much.

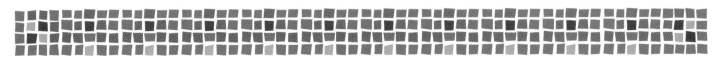

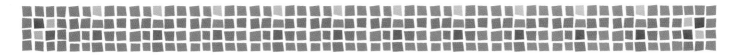

"Our temple in Nazareth is much smaller," Jesus told them. "And just before I left, the first lamb was born." He talked excitedly about his home for a while and then began to ask the elders some questions of his own. "How do you know if you are doing the things that God wants you to do?" asked Jesus.

"If you have faith in God and honor your parents, God will guide you to make the right decisions," replied one of the elders.

"I will keep trying to do those things," said Jesus. He continued to ask them other questions about Passover and Jerusalem. "I like it here very much," said Jesus. "I think I would like to live in Jerusalem some day." Jesus talked with the elders until it grew very late.

Mary did not think too much of Jesus being absent at first. With all of the families together it was hard to keep track of all of the children, who spent most of their time playing in the pastures outside the city. She knew he would be at the last meal of Passover. When Mary realized he was not there, though, she was concerned.

Mary asked the other children, "Have any of you seen Jesus?" But none of them had seen him, either. Mary and Joseph became worried. Finally, Mary decided to look at the temple at the end of the street. She entered the temple to find the elders gathered around Jesus.

"Mother, why did you worry?" asked Jesus. "Did you not know that I would be in my Father's house?"

Mary was so relieved to see Jesus that she found it hard to be angry with him. One of the elders took Mary aside. "You have been blessed," he said. "Your son will grow up to teach many people great things."

JOHN THE BAPTIST

Adapted by Elizabeth Olson

Illustrated by Teddy Edinjiklian

Early one morning, Daniel and Matthew's mother called to them, "Boys, please get up. Something very special is happening today."

"Can't we sleep just a little longer?" asked Daniel, yawning.

Matthew noticed that his mother was already dressed. "What is happening today?" he asked.

"John the Baptist is baptizing people in the River Jordan," she said. "Let's hurry so we can see him."

As the sleepy boys rolled up their sleeping mat, they asked, "Who is John the Baptist?"

"John the Baptist is one of God's servants," said their mother. "He baptizes us to wash away our sins."

Excited about the journey, the boys ate a breakfast of bread and dates, strapped on their sandals, and were ready to go.

Matthew and Daniel held their mother's hands as they walked to the River Jordan. The road was busier than usual, as hundreds of people walked in the same direction. Everyone was in a hurry.

"Look!" said Matthew. "I see the baker from the market. And over there is the woman who sells baskets."

"Do you see that man up ahead?" added Daniel. "He is riding a camel with two humps!"

"He must have come from far away," said their mother.

The crowd grew as it approached the River Jordan. Many people gathered along the river's edge. The boys and their mother drew close to the shore, but the boys could not see anything. Matthew and Daniel tried to peer between people's legs. They craned their necks and squinted their eyes. Despite their efforts, they could only glimpse the feet of the man speaking to everyone. Finally, with their mother's permission, they crawled to the front of the crowd for a better view.

Facing the people was a strong man dressed in simple clothes. The man smiled at Daniel and Matthew as the two boys sat on the ground. Daniel looked at the man's plain robe and twine belt. He whispered to his brother, "Is that John the Baptist?"

"I think so," answered Matthew.

Just then the baker stepped forward. John the Baptist led him into the river until the water was waist-high. As John the Baptist gently pushed the baker's head under the water, he said, "In the name of God, I baptize you." Then the baker came out of the water, wet but smiling.

"Yes, that must be John the Baptist," said Matthew to his brother. "He does not need to wear fine clothes to be important."

A stranger waded into the river. He stopped in front of John the Baptist. John the Baptist fell to his knees and bowed his head. The stranger put his hand on John the Baptist's shoulder. Then the boys recognized the stranger.

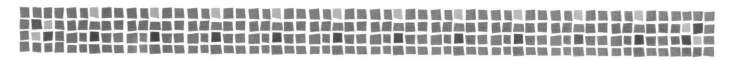

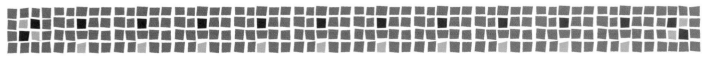

"It is Jesus!" they shouted. Jesus smiled at the boys.

"John the Baptist must be important if Jesus is his friend," whispered Daniel. The crowd grew quiet as everyone listened to Jesus.

"John," said Jesus. "I would like you to baptize me."

"But Jesus," said John the Baptist, with his head still bowed low, "I am not worthy of such a task. You are the one who should baptize me."

"God chose you," said Jesus. "He thinks you are very special."

Understanding God's will, John the Baptist humbly put his hand on Jesus' head and said, "In the name of God, I baptize you." Then he gently pushed Jesus' head into the river. At once a ray of sun broke through the clouds, and a warm wind blew. Dripping wet, Jesus emerged from the water and said, "Thank you, John."

"I am happy to do God's will," said John the Baptist.

A beautiful white bird landed on Jesus' shoulder. Jesus smiled at the boys again and said, "God sent this dove because he is very pleased that I have been baptized. He loves me just as he loves you."

The crowd started to move into the water toward John the Baptist.

"Come with me, boys," said Daniel and Matthew's mother. "The time has come for us to be baptized."

Smiling, Daniel and Matthew took their mother's hands and walked with her into the river.

THE TWELVE DISCIPLES

Adapted by Leslie Lindecker

Illustrated by Kallen Godsey

A girl named Sarah lived with her mother and father near the Sea of Galilee. One day, Sarah's parents were very excited. They told her that the whole family would be going to the seashore to hear a teacher speak. Sarah's father said he had heard many great things about this man called Jesus.

When they got to the Sea of Galilee, many people were gathered there. Jesus climbed onto a fishing boat. The fishermen were cleaning their nets on the shore.

"Simon Peter," Jesus said to one of the fishermen, "please take me out onto the water."

As Simon Peter rowed the boat out a short distance, everyone on the shore sat down to listen to Jesus speak. Sarah sat in her father's lap.

Jesus talked for a long time. He told wonderful stories Sarah could understand. Everyone around Sarah and her family kept very quiet so they could hear everything Jesus said.

After Jesus finished speaking, he turned to Simon Peter and said, "Cast your nets and catch fish to feed all these people."

Simon Peter said, "Teacher, we fished all night, but we did not catch any fish. If you wish, we will try again."

Simon Peter returned Jesus to the shore and then went back out to sea to cast his nets. At once the nets were full of fish! The nets were so heavy with fish, Simon Peter was afraid they might break. He waved at his partners James and John. James and John rowed a second boat out and helped pull the nets up into the two boats.

James, John, and Simon Peter rowed the boats back to the shore. Sarah's father and the other men on the shore helped them unload all the fish so everyone would have something to eat.

Jesus spoke to Simon Peter, James, and John. "You have been good fishermen," he said. "Now I want you to come with me and be fishers of men, helping me teach everyone about God."

Later that week, Sarah's father came home very excited. He told the family that Jesus had come to the village where Sarah and her family lived. Jesus met with the priests at the temple.

Outside the temple, a tax collector named Matthew was taking taxes from the people coming out of the temple. Jesus went up to Matthew and said, "Follow me."

Matthew walked away from his tax booth, leaving behind the money he had collected. They went to Matthew's home, where Jesus ate dinner with Matthew and his friends.

The priests were unhappy. They grumbled about Jesus choosing a tax collector to follow him. They said Matthew was the worst kind of sinner, and they were surprised that Jesus would eat with sinners.

Jesus said to them, "I call all people to follow me. Remember, God loves everyone, including the sinners and the tax collectors. They are the lost sheep who need God's love most of all."

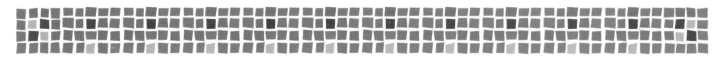

Sarah's family learned that Jesus was traveling to each of the towns and villages. He spoke in the temples all day. At dusk the people from these villages would come to Jesus to be healed by him and hear his wonderful stories. People traveled far to see Jesus.

Sarah's mother said, "Jesus tells us that we are like sheep without a shepherd. He says that he is the shepherd sent by God to gather the flock of sheep close to God."

"Jesus went up to the mountain to pray and has chosen twelve men to help him teach," said Sarah's father. "He chose Simon Peter, James, and John, the fishermen we saw at the Sea of Galilee. Jesus also chose Matthew the tax collector and men named Philip, Bartholomew, Judas, and Andrew. There are men from other villages named Thomas, James, and Simon. Some call Simon a zealot because he gets so excited. The last man is named Judas Iscariot."

These men traveled wherever Jesus went. They helped him teach everyone about the love of God.

Jesus invited all of his followers to join him and his disciples. Sarah and her family sat and listened quietly as Jesus spoke to his disciples.

"You will have the power to heal the sick, cleanse the spirit, and chase away demons," Jesus said to the men. "Seek the lost sheep of my Father's world and lead them back to his love. As you go, tell them, 'The kingdom of heaven is at hand,' and they will know you have been sent by the Son of God."

Jesus instructed his disciples, and together they were able to teach everyone about the love of God.

JESUS WELCOMES THE CHILDREN

Adapted by Elizabeth Olson

Illustrated by Holly Jones

Jonathan hummed a happy song while his little sister, Sarah, skipped along. They were very excited. They were going with their mother to see Jesus.

"Mother, where does Jesus live?" asked Jonathan.

"Does he have his own bedroom?" asked Sarah.

"Jesus lives in God's house," answered their mother. "God's house has enough rooms for everyone."

"Does God's house have a special place for dogs?" asked Jonathan, thinking of his best friend, a puppy that lived near the well.

Jonathan's mother laughed and said, "I don't know. You will have to ask Jesus, although I think I know the answer."

They arrived at the place where Jesus was meeting with his disciples. Other families were there to see Jesus too.

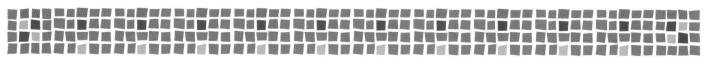

JESUS WELCOMES THE CHILDREN

Jonathan and Sarah pulled their mother up to the circle of disciples, who were now surrounded by families. Jonathan, who had recently grown, stood on his toes, but he could not see. Sarah peeked around the disciples' legs. Neither child could see Jesus.

"Mother," said Sarah, "can we please try to get closer? How will Jesus know we are here if he cannot see us?"

Jonathan began to worry. He said to his mother, "What if Jesus does not want to meet us? Maybe he is too busy to talk to children."

"Do not worry," said their mother. "Jesus has time for you. He knows that you are here even if you do not see him."

With their mother's permission, Jonathan and Sarah tried to squeeze past the disciples. The strings on one disciple's robe tickled Sarah's nose and made her giggle.

"Shhh," Jonathan whispered. "Let's not get into trouble."

Sarah did her best, but she could not help laughing again, very loudly. She put her hand over her mouth. Jonathan gave her a disapproving look.

"Hello, little girl. What are you doing down there?" a disciple in a yellow robe said to Sarah. He had a friendly smile.

"My brother, Jonathan, and I are here to meet Jesus," said Sarah.

"I am sorry, children," said the disciple. "Jesus is very busy today. He does not have time to meet you."

"But I have a question for him," said Jonathan. "I want to find out if God's house has room for my dog."

"You will have to ask him another day," said the disciple kindly.

Jesus overheard what the disciple said. "Do not tell the boy to leave," he said. "Let all the little children come to me."

JESUS WELCOMES THE CHILDREN

Jesus asked Jonathan and Sarah to sit with him. Then Jesus called out to the many people seated beyond the disciples. "Let all the children come forward," said Jesus. "I have something important to tell them."

Jesus sat on a rock and lifted Jonathan onto his knee. Sarah sat at Jesus' feet. Many other children gathered around.

Smiling at the children, Jesus said, "Little ones, you can approach me at any time. I am always here for you, because I love you."

Then Jesus said to the disciples, "The kingdom of heaven belongs to these children. Unless you are as trusting and open as they are, you will have no chance of entering God's house."

"Jesus, will you tell us more about God's house?" asked Jonathan quietly. "Is there room for dogs?"

Smiling, Jesus patted Jonathan's head. "Yes, son, there is room in God's house for all his creatures, big and small," said Jesus.

Many of the children had questions for Jesus. One boy wanted to know where the sun goes at night. Jesus told him that the sun waits in heaven. A little girl asked why trees are so tall. Jesus said that the trees reach for heaven. When the questions finally ended, Jesus rose and blessed each child.

"Jesus," said Sarah, "I have one more question. Will you walk home with us to our house?"

"Yes," Jesus answered. He took Sarah's and Jonathan's hands in his own. "Remember that I always have time for you."

THE FIRST MIRACLE

Adapted by Elizabeth Olson

Illustrated by Lynda Calvert-Weyant

Jesus, his disciples, and his mother, Mary, attended a grand wedding in Galilee. The guests were enjoying the festive celebration. They danced, laughed, and ate delicious spiced cakes. When they were thirsty, servants brought them goblets of wine from big stone jugs.

Mary was one of the happiest guests. She was happy to be near Jesus. She loved to watch him speaking with his new disciples. They were talking about God's love.

When Jesus had finished speaking with his disciples, the disciples left Jesus alone with his mother.

Mary said, "Jesus, I am so proud of you for spreading the word of God. You are a blessing to his name."

"Thank you," said Jesus. "I hope to be a blessing to you too."

"You have been a blessing to me since you were born," said Mary. "And I know that you have many more blessings to offer."

The musicians started to play a joyful song. The guests jumped up to dance. Jesus said, "Mother, will you dance with me?"

"Oh, yes," said Mary, beaming.

Jesus and Mary joined the other guests dancing around the bride and groom. Everyone clapped and laughed. When the song ended, the dancers were very thirsty. They asked the servants to refill their wine goblets, but the servants discovered that the stone jugs were empty.

"My friends," said the host, "I am sorry, but I have no more wine to give you. I have nothing left but water."

The guests were very disappointed.

Mary led Jesus by the hand to the host. "Jesus can make more wine," she said. "Please ask the servants to do whatever he requests."

Seeing Mary's faith in her son, the host agreed.

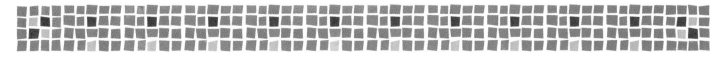

The disciples John and Philip watched Jesus curiously. They loved him, but they did not yet have complete faith in him. "Can Jesus turn water into wine?" whispered John.

"I do not know," answered Philip. "Turning water into wine is a miracle. If Jesus can do this, we must follow him wherever he goes."

Mary knew that Jesus could do it. Jesus said to the servants, "Please fill these empty jugs with water."

The servants dashed to the nearby well and pumped water into every available pail, bottle, bowl, and cup. Spilling water as they went, they ran back to Jesus, poured water into the jugs, and hurried back to the well for more. Finally, each jug was filled to the brim.

One servant eagerly turned to Jesus and asked, "What do you want us to do next?"

Everyone waited for Jesus to reply.

THE FIRST MIRACLE

205

Jesus turned to a girl, one of the youngest servants, and said to her, "Please pour a goblet of water for the wedding host."

The host stood near Jesus as he waited. A bit nervous, the girl chose a fine stone goblet from the table. She carefully filled the goblet and handed it to the host. He took a long drink while all the guests held their breath. Then he looked at the goblet in disbelief.

"Delicious!" he shouted. "This is the best wine I have ever tasted."

"Hooray!" shouted the servants and all the guests.

"Praise be to God! It is a miracle!" shouted Philip and John.

"Bless you, son," said Mary quietly. "I knew you could do it."

The happy host asked the servants to serve the wine. "Let everyone rejoice in this miracle!" he shouted, raising his goblet. "God has blessed us on this special wedding day."

Everyone celebrated the first miracle of Jesus. The guests laughed, danced, ate, and drank some more. Now, with God's blessing, the festivities were even happier.

Mary hugged Jesus. "This miracle is a sign from God of his love for you and all of us," she said. "As you grow, I know that my love for you will also grow as you do many more wonderful things."

Mary turned her face to heaven and said, "Thank you, God, for my son."

SOWING SEEDS

Adapted by Lisa Harkrader

Illustrated by Flora Jew

Hannah scrambled down the path after her mother. The aromas of sweet perfume and roasting meat drifted up from the market. Beyond the marketplace, the Sea of Galilee sparkled under the morning sun. Hannah's mother dropped some coins into Hannah's hand.

"Are you sure you feel comfortable going to the market on your own?" Hannah's mother asked.

"Yes, Mama," said Hannah. "I am sure."

"Do not go near the meat seller," said her mother. "He mistreats his workers. We won't reward him by buying his meat. Try to buy eggs at a good price, but do not take advantage of the egg seller's kindness."

"Yes, Mama." Hannah sighed. Going to the market would be more fun if she did not have so many rules to follow.

The market was crowded, but soon people headed toward the sea. They were following a man who was telling stories as he walked.

Hannah loved stories. She held her basket tight and followed the crowd. Everyone stopped at the edge of the sea. The man who was telling stories climbed up onto a boat so everyone could see him.

Hannah was standing beside an old woman. She tugged on the woman's robe and pointed to the man on the boat.

"Who is he?" Hannah asked.

"His name is Jesus," said the woman, smiling. "His stories open our eyes and show us the truth. They show us God's word in a new way."

Jesus looked out over the crowd. His face was filled with kindness. He began speaking. "A farmer went out to sow his seeds. As he was scattering the seeds, some fell along the path, and birds ate them up."

Hannah nodded. That happened once when she helped her father plant wheat. She had spilled a few seeds on the path. Birds ate the seeds before she could pick them up.

Hannah listened as Jesus continued. "Some seeds fell on rocky places, where they did not have much soil. Plants sprang up quickly, because the soil was shallow. But when the sun came up, the plants were scorched, and they withered."

Hannah frowned. Her father told her not to plant seeds in rocky patches. The plants would not get enough water. They would not have enough soil under them to grow deep roots. Any farmer knew that. When would Jesus get to the new part of the story?

Jesus continued speaking. "Other seeds fell among thorns," he said, "which grew up and choked the plants."

Hannah tugged on the old woman's robe again. "That is not a new story," she said. "Why does everyone think Jesus is so wise?"

The woman smiled. "Keep listening," she said.

Hannah shook her head, but she kept listening.

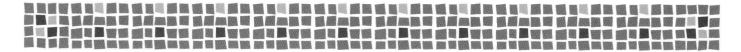

"Still other seeds fell on good soil," said Jesus. "Plants sprung up, grew, and yielded a crop a hundred times more than was planted."

Jesus stopped speaking. Hannah waited. Was the story over? She looked around. Others in the crowd seemed confused, too. One man asked what the story meant.

Jesus explained, "The seed is the word of God. Those along the path hear the word, but the devil comes and takes the word from their hearts, so they may not believe and be saved. Those on the rock receive the word with joy, but they have no roots. They believe for a while, but when trouble comes because of the word, they fall away. Those among thorns hear the word, but then they are choked by life's worries, riches, and pleasures, and they do not grow. But the seeds on the good soil have a noble and good heart. They hear the word, keep it, and produce a crop."

Hannah smiled. The woman was right. Jesus' story had shown her God's word in a new way.

Hannah ran back toward the market. She found her mother at the carpet weaver's stall and called, "Mama! I understand."

Her mother looked up. "You understand what, Hannah?"

"I understand your rules," Hannah said. "You want me to know right from wrong, so that when I hear God's word, it will not blow away. You want me to have the courage to stand up for God's word. And you want me to put God's word ahead of money and greed."

Hannah laughed. "You want me to have good soil!"

THE GOOD SAMARITAN

Adapted by Leslie Lindecker

Illustrated by Janet Jones

One day Jesus was teaching in the temple. A young man stood and asked, "Teacher, what do I have to do to get into heaven?"

Jesus said to the young man, "What do the scriptures tell you?"

The man answered, "I have studied the word of God. It says to love God with all your heart, your soul, your strength, and your mind. It also says to love your neighbor as you love yourself."

"That is right," replied Jesus. "If you do these things, you can trust that you will get into heaven."

"But teacher, who is my neighbor?" the man asked.

Jesus decided to help the man understand by telling him a story.

Jesus began, "Once there was a man who was walking from Jerusalem to Jericho. Along the way, some robbers took his clothes and everything he had. The man fell beside the road and cried."

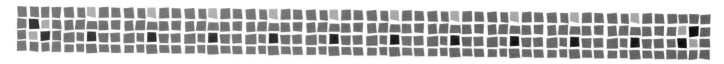

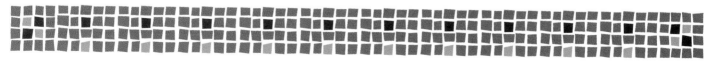

"A priest from the temple in Jerusalem came by on his donkey. The priest saw the man on the side of the road but had other important things on his mind and did not want to take the time to help. The priest also did not want to get his robes dirty, so he pretended not to see the man and ignored his calls for help.

"A second man came by later that day. He was also a religious man, an assistant to the priests in the temple. The assistant saw the man beside the road and was afraid to help him. He worried that the robbers might be nearby. What if they robbed him next? He decided that it was too risky. The assistant crossed the road and hurried past the man lying on the ground.

"The poor man wept bitter tears because the men from his own village would not help him. He was all alone, and tired, hurt, and sad. He did not think he could make it to Jericho by himself.

"Very late in the afternoon, another man came walking along the road with his donkey. This man was a Samaritan."

Jesus paused in his storytelling. He reminded everyone that many people from Jerusalem did not trust Samaritans. Jesus explained that Samaritans worshiped other gods and were considered different from the people of Jerusalem. He continued his story.

"This Samaritan saw the man lying by the road. The Samaritan did not see him as a man from Jerusalem or even as a stranger. He saw him only as a man who needed help. He felt compassion for the man. The Samaritan took off his cloak and draped it over the man to keep him warm. He knelt and wiped the dirt and dust from the man's face. He cleaned the man's bruises and cuts and bandaged them. He gave him water to drink. Finally, the Samaritan helped the man to his feet.

"The Samaritan told the man, 'We will go to the next inn and find you some food and a place to rest.' The Samaritan put his arm around the man and helped him onto his donkey.

"The man from Jerusalem was grateful for the stranger's kindness. He thanked the stranger again and again as they made their way."

THE GOOD SAMARITAN

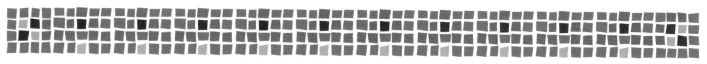

"The two men walked until they found an inn at the next town. The Samaritan paid the innkeeper for food and a room. He kept watch over the man from Jerusalem all night long. He made sure the man had enough to eat and drink. He sat quietly so the man could sleep.

"The next morning, the Samaritan went to the innkeeper and said, 'Here are some coins. Please watch over this man. He has had a difficult journey and needs our help. Be sure to give him plenty to eat and drink. Let him sleep until he feels well enough to continue his trip to Jericho. When I return, I will give you more coins to repay you for taking care of him.'

"The innkeeper agreed to take care of the man. The Samaritan left the inn to continue his journey. The innkeeper took care of the man from Jerusalem until he was well enough to travel again, and he made his way safely to Jericho."

When Jesus finished his story, he sat silently to let his listeners think about what he had said.

After a few moments, Jesus spoke to the young man who had first asked the question. Jesus said, "Which of the three travelers treated the man who was robbed as a neighbor? Was it the priest, the assistant, or the Samaritan?"

The young man answered Jesus. "The Samaritan showed kindness to the man even though they had never met before."

Jesus said, "Everyone should try to be like the good Samaritan. You must show kindness and mercy to each person you meet. They are all your neighbors, and you must love them as God has said."

JAIRUS' DAUGHTER

Adapted by Suzanne Lieurance

Illustrated by Amanda Haley

Long ago, there was a man named Jairus. Jairus was a church ruler, and he had a daughter whom he loved and cherished.

One day, Jairus' daughter was speaking with her friends about miracles. A boy said, "I do not know if I believe in miracles."

"Oh, I believe," said Jairus' daughter. "I am going to tell you about a miracle. I know this story very well, because I have heard my father tell it many times. This miracle happened to me.

"It happened when I was very sick. My father heard that Jesus would be preaching by the lake with his disciples. My father was afraid I would die, so he traveled to the lake. When he found Jesus, my father got down on his knees. He said that I was near death, and he asked Jesus to come heal me."

"What did Jesus say?" asked one of the friends.

"Jesus said he would come," said Jairus' daughter.

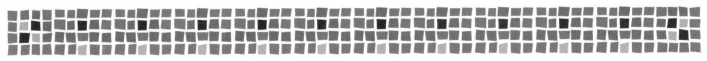

"Go on," said the boy. "What happened next?"

Jairus' daughter moved closer to her friends and went on with her story. "Jesus started to make his way to our house, but a huge crowd followed him. My father was getting worried, because Jesus could not move very quickly in the crowd. People kept stopping Jesus to talk to him, too. Then something amazing happened."

The children leaned forward. "What?" they all asked at once.

Jairus' daughter's eyes got very big, and her voice was almost a whisper. "A woman came up and touched the hem of Jesus' robe. The woman had touched him so lightly, Jesus did not even notice her. The woman was very sick, but as soon as she touched the robe she was healed.

"Jesus turned and asked who had touched him. The disciples said there was a large crowd, and many people had been brushing up against Jesus. Jesus could feel that he had healed someone."

"Did Jesus find out who had touched him?" asked one of the girls.

"Yes," said Jairus' daughter. "The woman came forward. She explained that Jesus had healed her."

"What did Jesus do then?" asked one of the girls.

"He was very kind to the woman," said Jairus' daughter. "He kept talking to her. Jesus told the woman that her faith had healed her. Just then, messengers arrived to tell my father that it was too late. His daughter was already dead."

The children gasped.

"No!" said one of them. "But it was not true. You are alive."

"Oh, but it was true," said Jairus' daughter. "I was dead, and my father was heartbroken. He collapsed with grief. But Jesus said, 'Do not be afraid. Just believe.' "

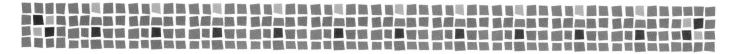

"Jesus and his disciples Peter, James, and John followed my grieving father to our house. My father was not in a hurry now because he thought it was too late to save me.

"As they approached the house, they could hear the wailing sounds of mourners. Neighbors were gathering to try to comfort my family. Jesus turned to the people and said, 'The child is not dead, but asleep.' But my father had seen death before, and he knew what it looked like. My father could not understand why Jesus kept insisting that I was still alive. Everyone knew that even great healers could not bring the dead back to life.

"Jesus turned to my father and told him that everyone must leave. 'You, your wife, and my disciples may stay,' said Jesus.

"Everyone left the house, then Jesus walked over to the bed and said, 'Little girl, I say to you, get up.' Immediately, I stood up and walked around. Everyone was astonished. Then Jesus hugged me and asked if I wanted something to eat."

Jairus' daughter looked at her friends, who were all staring at her in awe. They were happy that their friend was alive.

"So you see," she said, "Jesus takes care of all the little children like us. He even performed a miracle so I could live."

"Yes, that was truly a miracle," said a boy.

"I am grateful that Jesus performed this miracle," said Jairus' daughter. "And I am grateful that everyone who hears my story will believe in miracles, too."

JESUS WALKS ON WATER

Adapted by Rebecca Grazulis

Illustrated by Pamela Johnson

At sunrise, Jesus and his disciples set out to share a message of peace. Jesus enjoyed talking to all different kinds of people, young and old, rich and poor. He was very grateful for his disciples' help. When the sun began to set, Jesus led them to a boat.

"Friends, thank you for teaching with me today," said Jesus. "You must be tired. Please use this boat to go to Capernaum and rest."

The disciples did not want to leave Jesus, but they agreed. It had been a long day. They got into the boat and prepared to set sail.

"Won't you come with us, Jesus?" asked Peter. "You must be tired also. Let's all go together."

"Do not worry, Peter," replied Jesus. "I will meet you later. It is important that you rest for our work tomorrow."

The disciples trusted that Jesus knew what was best. They waved goodbye and pushed the boat away from the shore.

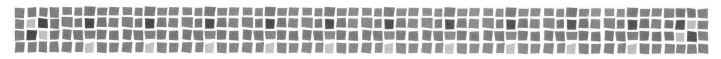

Jesus watched the disciples' boat sail across the Sea of Galilee. He thought about how lucky he was to have such good friends.

"They will help me on my journey," thought Jesus, "and I will show them how much God loves them."

Soon, Jesus wanted to find a quiet place where he could talk to his Father. He decided to climb to the top of a hill, where he kneeled and began to pray.

"Dear Father," he said, "please show me how I can best serve you."

Suddenly, the sky grew as dark as night, and the wind began to whip through the hills. Jesus thought of his friends traveling on the Sea of Galilee. He searched the horizon and spotted the small boat moving slowly towards Capernaum. The disciples were safe for now, but the darkness and wind were signs that a storm was coming. Jesus began to worry about his friends. He knew that they would face trouble during the storm.

The disciples were starting to think they might be in danger. The sky had turned black, and they could no longer see into the distance. They rowed and rowed, but Capernaum was still far away.

"I am afraid we will not be able to reach the shore," Peter said.

The other disciples tried to comfort Peter, but they were also troubled. What would happen if they lost their way? Who could help them?

Soon the wind grew stronger. The waves became so tall that they crashed over the sides of the boat. Now the disciples were wet and tired. It was starting to look like they might never get to Capernaum.

The disciples tried to be brave. "We must have faith!" they cried.

From high on the hill, Jesus saw the small boat being tossed and turned in the mighty waves. He knew the disciples needed his help. He quickly ran down the hill toward the water.

When he reached the shore, Jesus gently placed his foot on top of the water. Soon he was walking on the water toward the boat.

Early in the morning, the disciples saw a man walking toward them on the water. They could not believe their eyes. Frightened, they yelled, "It's a ghost!"

"Do not be afraid," Jesus said. "It is your friend Jesus."

Peter was not sure whether it was really Jesus. "Lord, if it is really you," Peter said, "ask me to walk on the water."

"All right," said Jesus. "Come, and I will wait for you here."

Peter stepped over the side of the boat. Slowly, he steadied himself and walked on the water toward Jesus. Peter only had taken a few steps when he saw the tall waves crashing around him. Peter got scared. He could not move any farther and fell into the water. Peter cried out for Jesus to help him.

Jesus rescued Peter. The two men climbed into the boat. Peter thanked Jesus.

Jesus replied, "You need to have more faith, Peter. Trust in God."

Suddenly, the disciples realized that the wind had stopped and the water was calm. Before long, they reached the shore.

The people of Capernaum soon met the disciples. Everyone wanted to hear the story of their amazing trip. Jesus was happy. He would teach them all about the importance of faith.

THE LITTLE FISHERMAN

Adapted by Megan Musgrave

Illustrated by Diane Paterson

Martin was a little boy who lived in a small fishing village on the shore of the Sea of Galilee. Everyone in his family worked hard. Martin's father was a fisherman. He and Martin's older brothers spent each day catching fish to sell in the town market. Martin's job was to untangle the fishing nets. He also helped his mother at home, making bread to sell in the market.

For a boy, fishing and baking were not always fun. Martin wished he could play more often. One day he snuck away to the village, where the old men were talking about someone named Jesus. Jesus performed miracles and people came from all over to see him, the old men said. Martin asked them, "Who is Jesus?"

"He is a teacher from Nazareth who has been traveling around, speaking to people and performing miracles," old Nathaniel said.

Abe added, "Jesus and his disciples are resting for a few days several miles down the shore, and some people from the village want to go and see him."

Martin wanted to see Jesus perform a miracle. He rushed home and asked his parents if he could go to see Jesus. His parents said no, because they all had too much work to do. That night, Martin decided he would make the journey anyway, by himself. He filled his satchel with a few fish and loaves of bread so he would not get hungry on his long walk.

Early the next morning, Martin set off down the sea shore. By early afternoon, Martin finally reached the place where Jesus and his disciples had stopped to rest.

Martin was amazed to see thousands of people gathered there. He looked around and saw a bunch of people clustered around a gentle-looking man. Soon Jesus started to speak to the crowd. He talked for a long time about being kind to others and treating them the way you want to be treated yourself.

Martin thought about his family. "I guess I have not been a very good son," he said to himself.

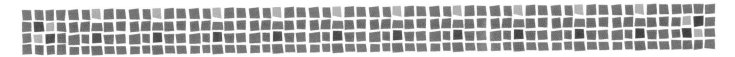

After some time, Martin heard people say they were hungry. Most people had eaten all their food on the road. It was too far to walk back to the village for food. Martin had five loaves of bread and two fish left over, but he knew it would not be enough to feed everyone. Also, if he shared his food with other people, he would not have enough left for his long walk home.

When he thought about home, Martin realized how selfish it had been for him to leave without telling his family. If he could not tell them he was sorry at that moment, at least he could do something nice for someone else.

Martin walked up to Jesus and said, "You can take the food I have left. It will not be enough to feed this big crowd, but please give it to someone who needs it more than I do."

"You have a kind heart, Martin," said Jesus. "Do not worry. God always provides enough for those who give to others. Will you please help me pass out the food?"

Martin was honored to help Jesus. Jesus said a prayer over the food, and then Martin carried the satchel for him as they walked through the crowd. People held up their food baskets, and Jesus broke off pieces of bread and fish and filled the baskets. Every time Jesus reached into the satchel, he pulled out more food. Soon Jesus had given bread and fish to every person there, and there was even more food left over!

"How did you feed so many people, Jesus?" Martin asked.

"There is no end to the generosity you can find in your heart, Martin," Jesus replied.

Martin was amazed and relieved that his own little food satchel had provided so much for so many people. He was excited to be part of a miracle, but he was even happier about how the miracle made him feel. He had spent so much time doing what he wanted that he never realized how wonderful it felt to give to others.

Before he set off on the road home, Martin thanked Jesus.

"And thank you, Martin, for sharing your kindness with us," answered Jesus.

Martin got home very late. His whole family was worried but very happy to see him. Martin apologized for worrying them. Then he told them about the miracle Jesus had performed.

"The best part about the miracle was the good feeling it gave me to share with everyone else," Martin said. "I never knew how nice it is to think about other people instead of myself. I have not been a very good son or brother, but I promise to be more helpful from now on."

THE LOST SHEEP

Adapted by Lora Kalkman

Illustrated by Rosanne Litzinger

One day Jesus was walking through a bustling town. Soon he stopped to talk with all of the people who were there.

Jesus talked with the shopkeepers, even though some did not treat their customers fairly. He talked with the construction workers, even though some rested when they should have been working. He even talked to the tax collectors who unjustly took money from people who needed it. Jesus knew that many of the townspeople did things that were wrong. Still, he smiled and talked to everyone.

Other people were upset by this. They thought Jesus should talk only with them, because they tried hard to obey God.

"Why does Jesus talk with those sinners?" one woman asked. "He should not waste time with them. They are not good people, like us."

Jesus heard the people talking. He explained that he did not think he was wasting his time at all. Then he gathered the people around him and told them this parable.

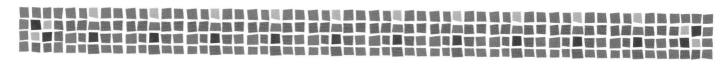

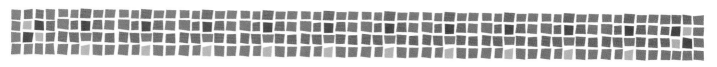

"Once there was a young shepherd boy who played his small wooden flute while tending to his sheep. In the morning, the sheep would awake to the flute's soft, sweet melodies. Happily, the shepherd led his sheep out to pasture. The sheep grazed on the bright green grass, wet with morning dew.

"In the afternoon, when the sun grew hot, the boy would herd his sheep to a shady spot to rest. The shepherd boy would always sit nearby and play the flute. The sheep adored the delightful music. They gladly gathered around their beloved shepherd.

"As the shepherd boy played, he lovingly gazed at his one hundred sheep. Each one was unique. Curly liked to snuggle next to his mother. Patch had a black spot on her chest. Daisy liked to lie near the old wooden fence. The shepherd boy knew that each and every sheep was special, and he cherished them all. He had seen all their births, took care of them when they were sick, and comforted them when they were frightened. The boy took great care to make sure every sheep was safe and comfortable."

"Every night, the shepherd boy lulled his flock to sleep with melodies from his flute. The sheep would listen contentedly, happily gathered around their master as they drifted off into peaceful slumber.

"One night, when the flock was asleep, the boy gently placed his flute in its case and got ready for bed. It had been a long, hot day, and the boy was tired. He was looking forward to a good night's sleep.

"Before going to sleep, the shepherd boy walked among his sheep to make sure they were all right. One by one, the shepherd boy said goodnight to his flock. He soon realized that Lilly, one of the lambs, was missing. He called for her and searched, but he could not find her.

" 'Perhaps if I play my flute, Lilly will hear it and find her way back home,' the boy thought. He got his flute and began to play softly, but Lilly did not come home.

"Confident that the rest of the flock was safe, the shepherd boy set out in search of his little lost lamb."

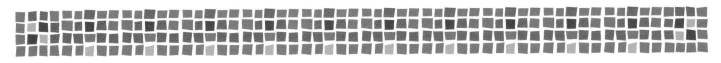

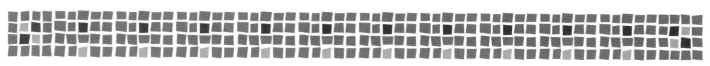

"The shepherd boy knew that little sheep sometimes strayed from the flock, but he refused to lose even one. He vowed to search until he found her.

"The shepherd boy looked everywhere. He walked out to the grassy pastures where the sheep grazed when they were hungry. He heard some crickets in the night, but there was no sign of Lilly.

"The shepherd boy ventured farther into the wooded lands beyond, where the sheep liked to rest when they were hot. He heard an old hoot owl singing in the night, but still there was no sign of Lilly.

" 'Lilly!' he called. 'Lilly, where are you? I love you very much and want you to come home.'

"Just then, the shepherd boy turned and saw Lilly shivering in the cool night air, all alone. Lilly and the boy ran to each other, and he hugged her tightly. The boy was so happy to see her again. He could never be angry at one of his lost sheep."

" 'I am so glad I found you,' he assured Lilly. 'I was so worried. I know that little lambs sometimes stray from the flock, but never fear. I will always find you and forgive you, because I love you.'

"With that, he lifted Lilly upon his shoulders and carried her home. When they reached the stable, he gently laid the little lamb down to sleep. Once again, he gazed over his flock to make sure all one hundred sheep were there. When he knew that each one was home, the shepherd boy smiled. His flock was now safe, and he could finally rest.

"The shepherd boy loved all his sheep, just as God loves all people."

THE PRODIGAL SON

Adapted by Lora Kalkman

Illustrated by Beth Foster Wiggins

Once there was a man who lived on a large estate with his two sons. This man was a very successful farmer. After working hard all his life, he was finally able to hire servants to help.

Although the man had become quite wealthy, he still worked hard. He insisted that his sons work hard too. Together, they and their servants tended to the crops and livestock. The older son did not mind working hard. He gladly helped with the chores around the farm. The younger son, however, did not like working at all.

"Why must we work so hard?" he asked his father. "We are very wealthy. We have servants. We should not have to work in the fields."

"Son," his father explained, "our farm has grown large and prosperous because of our work. Success comes to those who earn it."

The younger son replied that he did not want to work anymore. He asked his father for his share of the family's money. Then, to his father's dismay, the younger son left to see the world.

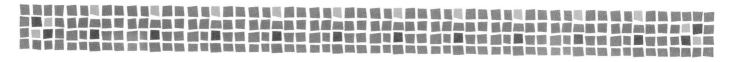

The young man was excited to leave the farm. Gleefully, he counted the gold coins in the bag his father had given him.

"There are so many," he said with delight. "I have enough money to visit the grandest cities and shop in the finest stores."

The young man journeyed to the largest city in the land. When he arrived, he found a very fancy place to live, with silk curtains and velvet furniture. He ate at the best restaurants, feasted on fine foods every night of the week and wore the most expensive clothes. If he saw something he wanted, he bought it without even a second thought.

"My father and brother are fools," he said to himself. "They are foolish to spend their days working hard in the fields. They should be enjoying their money like me."

The young man never considered getting a job. After all, he still had plenty of gold in his bag. Even though his father tried to teach him the value of hard work, the young man refused to learn the lesson.

One day while the young man was shopping, a belt caught his eye. "I would like to purchase that belt," he told the shopkeeper.

The young man opened his bag to pay the shopkeeper. It was only then that he realized all of his gold was gone!

"How can this be?" he shrieked in despair. "There were so many coins when I came to the city. Could I really have spent them all?"

Alas, the young man had spent his entire fortune on fancy clothes and jewels and things he did not need. Now he had nothing. He did not even have one coin to buy a loaf of bread.

The young man walked to a nearby farm and got a job working in the fields. He had to work very hard on the farm. He did not make very much money, and he often went to bed hungry.

"If I am going to work, I might as well go home and work for my father," he decided. "Maybe then I will at least have enough to eat."

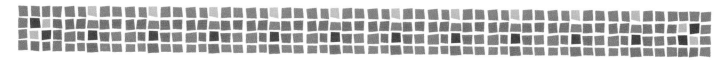

The young man returned to his father's home. As he approached the gate, he felt nervous. He knew he had been wrong. Instead of working hard as his father had taught him, he had wasted all of his money on unimportant things. He was so afraid his father would be angry that he considered turning back. Then he saw his father running toward him. To the young man's surprise, his father smiled and stretched his arms out for a hug.

"Dear son," his father said. "I am so glad you have come back. I have missed you so much."

The father was so happy his younger son had returned that he threw a big party to celebrate. He gave his son a new robe and shoes. He gave him all of the farm's best food to eat.

The older son did not understand. He grew angry. He did not think his father should treat his younger brother so well. After all, he had been good and worked hard while his brother had behaved very badly.

The father noticed his older son's unhappiness. "Why are you upset?" he asked. "Aren't you happy that your brother is home?"

"Why are you so good to my brother?" the older son replied. "I do not think it is fair."

The father hugged his older son. "Your brother sees his mistakes. We must forgive and love each other, as God loves and forgives us."

The young man considered his father's wise words. Then he turned to embrace his younger brother. "Welcome home," he said.

ZACCHAEUS

Adapted by Suzanne Lieurance

Illustrated by Jim McConnell

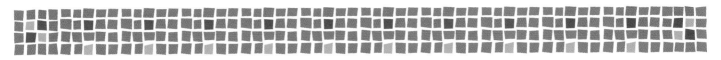

Once there was a man named Zacchaeus who lived in the city of Jericho. Zacchaeus was very short. He was also extremely wealthy. He wore the finest clothes and the most beautiful jewelry.

In spite of his nice clothes and jewelry, no one in Jericho liked Zacchaeus. The people knew that he stole money—*their* money. Zacchaeus was a tax collector, and each time he came to collect taxes he took more money than the people owed. That way, he could keep plenty of money for himself.

As Zacchaeus walked down the streets of Jericho each morning, in his fine clothes and beautiful jewelry, he looked different from the people he passed. They looked poor. Their clothes were tattered, and they had no beautiful jewelry. But they had one thing Zacchaeus did not have. They had happiness. The people had friends and family that cared about them. The poor people even smiled a lot.

Zacchaeus could not remember the last time he smiled. He did not have any friends. Zacchaeus believed that he did not need happiness.

ZACCHAEUS

One day, as Zacchaeus was walking down the street, he heard some men talking.

"Jesus is coming to town," said one of the men. "Let's hurry so we can go hear him preach."

The men seemed excited about hearing Jesus, so Zacchaeus wanted to hear him preach, too. He hurried after the men, but soon the streets were crowded with people who had gathered to hear Jesus.

Because Zacchaeus was so short, he could not see anything but the backs of other people. If he did not get through this crowd, he would never see Jesus or hear him preach. Zacchaeus tried to push his way through, but there were just too many people. He stood on his tiptoes, but that did not work either.

Finally, Zacchaeus heard Jesus' voice in the distance, coming toward him. The crowd had parted up ahead so Jesus could walk through. Zacchaeus was still pushing and shoving, trying to see Jesus.

Zacchaeus pushed and shoved until he was red in the face. But he did not seem to be getting anywhere. He still could not see a thing.

After a few minutes, he got an idea. If he had to be much taller to see Jesus above the crowd, then Zacchaeus would become much taller.

Zacchaeus walked over to a sturdy sycamore tree and reached up to one of its branches. He pulled himself up and stood on the bottom branch. That was not much better, though. Now, instead of seeing everyone's backs, he saw the backs of their heads. Zacchaeus needed to be taller still.

Zacchaeus stretched to grab a higher branch of the tree, then pulled himself up and stood on a strong limb. Ahh! Now he could see above everyone. He saw Jesus getting closer and closer.

As Jesus approached the sycamore tree where Zacchaeus was perched, the crowd parted again to let Jesus through. Soon Jesus was right below Zacchaeus.

ZACCHAEUS

ZACCHAEUS

Jesus stopped at the sycamore tree. He looked up at the finely dressed man perched on the big broad limb. No one even had to tell Jesus the name of this strange-looking little man with all the gold jewelry.

"Zacchaeus, please come down. I would like to go to your house," said Jesus. Jesus reached up to help Zacchaeus down from the tree.

Zacchaeus took Jesus' hand and climbed to the ground. The crowd gathered around the two men. Zacchaeus proudly smiled as he welcomed Jesus to Jericho, but Zacchaeus noticed that nobody else was smiling. In fact, they were talking about him.

People muttered to each other, "Jesus has gone to be the guest of a sinner. Why would he want to do that?"

Zacchaeus stood at his front door. He looked at all the people, with their tattered clothes and no jewelry. He decided he did not want to be greedy anymore.

"Lord," Zacchaeus said to Jesus, "I will give half of my possessions to the poor. If I have cheated anybody out of anything, I will pay back four times the amount."

Zacchaeus wanted Jesus to know that he was ready to change his life. He pulled some coins from his pocket and handed them to a man.

Jesus said, "God sent me so I could help you. Now he forgives you."

Zacchaeus had changed. Soon he would be a happy man.

THE LAST SUPPER

Adapted by Rebecca Grazulis

Illustrated by Allan Eitzen

When the day had come to celebrate the Passover, Jesus and his twelve disciples sat down to share their supper. Jesus became serious. "One of you will soon betray me," he warned the disciples.

The disciples were upset. "You do not mean me, Lord, do you?" each disciple asked in turn.

Judas Iscariot realized that Jesus knew it was he, Judas, who would betray him. Jesus, however did not openly accuse him. Instead, Jesus offered Judas the biggest and best helping of food.

Jesus was sad. He loved all of his disciples, even Judas, who would soon turn against him. Jesus raised a loaf of bread and asked God to bless it. He gave each man a piece, saying, "Eat this bread. It is my body given for you." Then Jesus raised his cup of wine. "Drink this," he said, "in remembrance of me."

Thoughtfully, the disciples ate and drank. The disciples did not understand what Jesus meant, but they saw how serious he was.

After the supper, Jesus took the disciples to a garden called Gethsemane. "Please wait here while I talk to my Father," said Jesus.

Jesus found a quiet spot and fell to his knees. "Dear God," he prayed, "I do not want to suffer. Please help me to be brave, so your will can be done."

When Jesus returned, he found the disciples sleeping. "Can you not keep your eyes open?" he asked. "The time has come for the will of God to be done. My betrayer is here!"

Judas arrived, leading a group of town leaders and guards who looked very angry. "Hello, teacher," Judas said as he kissed Jesus.

"Friends, do what you must do," said Jesus. "I know this is part of God's plan for my life."

Jesus also knew that the kiss was a signal for the guards. Suddenly, they grabbed Jesus and arrested him.

The guards escorted Jesus to Pontius Pilate, the Roman governor. Pilate asked Jesus, "Are you the King of the Jews?"

"Yes, it is true," replied Jesus.

He stood silently as the town leaders said, "This man believes he is a king. He believes he is divine."

Pilate was surprised that Jesus said nothing to defend himself. A crowd began to gather. The town leaders made everyone believe that Jesus should be punished. Soon, everyone was shouting, "Crucify him!"

"Why?" asked Pilate. "He has done nothing wrong!"

Pilate became very nervous. He could see that the crowd was growing bigger and more angry. He felt he had no choice. Finally, he said, "This man is innocent. If you wish to crucify him, it must be your responsibility, not mine!" Pilate ordered Jesus to be taken by the Roman soldiers and crucified.

The guards placed a crown of sharp thorns upon Jesus' head before leading him away to be crucified. As they walked, Jesus carried a heavy cross until they reached Golgotha, a tall hill. There, the guards nailed Jesus to the cross. They placed a sign above his head that said "Jesus, King of the Jews." There was a criminal hanging upon a cross to the left of Jesus, and another one to his right.

As Jesus hung on his cross, people came to shout at him. "If you are the Son of God, save yourself!" they cried. Even the priests mocked him, yelling, "Look at the king now!"

In the distance, many of Jesus' heartbroken friends watched, including Mary Magdalene. At noon, darkness covered the land. At three o'clock, Jesus called out with a strong voice, "My God, why have you forsaken me?"

When Jesus called out again, he died upon the cross. Suddenly, the earth began to shake, and rocks split in two. The Roman guards were scared by the earthquake. One said, "Truly, this was the Son of God!"

Joseph of Arimathea, a rich man who had loved Jesus, was upset over the death of his friend. He went to Pilate and asked, "Sir, may I have Jesus' body so I can give him a proper burial?"

Pilate agreed. Joseph returned to Golgotha and carefully wrapped Jesus' body in a long linen cloth. Mary Magdalene sat nearby, watching sadly. She followed Joseph as he carried Jesus to a tomb carved out of the rock in the side of a hill. Mary Magdalene and Joseph gently placed Jesus in the tomb and said goodbye. As they left, Joseph and his friend Nicodemus rolled a giant stone across the entrance of the tomb to protect Jesus' body. Jesus could now rest peacefully.

JESUS LIVES

Adapted by Brian Conway

Illustrated by Pamela Becker

After Jesus died, Mary Magdalene visited his tomb every morning. She felt very sad, and it made her feel good to pray by his tomb.

One morning as Mary Magdalene entered the garden, she stopped in surprise. She could not believe what she saw. The boulder that once covered the tomb had been pushed aside! "Oh!" she cried. "Someone has taken away Jesus' body!"

Mary Magdalene slowly crept up to the tomb and peered inside. The white cloth that had covered Jesus' body was lying on the floor. Jesus was missing.

What was left was a miraculous sight. Two angels dressed in white sat where Jesus' body used to be. The two angels looked calmly at Mary Magdalene. "Dear Mary, why are you crying?" the angels asked her.

"Someone has taken Jesus away," Mary answered through her tears. "I am frightened." Mary Magdalene shook her head in disbelief. She slowly backed away from the tomb.

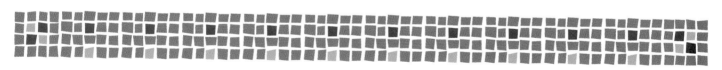

As Mary Magdalene turned, she bumped into a man. She was crying so hard she did not look up. She assumed that he might be the gardener. He asked her why she was crying.

"Please, sir," she said. "Do you know where Jesus has been taken?"

Because she was crying and she was very worried, Mary Magdalene did not recognize this man. He was a man she knew well. He was Jesus.

"Mary, do not cry," Jesus said softly. "It is me."

"Teacher! You are alive!" she cried. She reached out to hug him.

"Do not hold on to me," Jesus said, "because I have not returned to my Father yet. Instead, go and tell my disciples that I have returned. Tell them I will see them before I return to my Father."

Mary Magdalene did as Jesus told her. She rushed to see Jesus' disciples, and she told them what had happened.

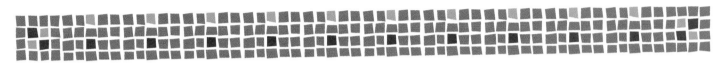

That night the disciples went fishing together in the Sea of Galilee. They had listened carefully to what Mary Magdalene had told them. The disciples missed Jesus and were very excited about his return. They wondered when Jesus would appear to them.

"He did not tell Mary Magdalene when," said Simon Peter. "He only said he would return to us."

The men fished through the night but did not catch anything. Early in the morning, a man on the distant shore called to them.

"Friends," the man said, "your nets are empty. Why haven't you caught any fish?"

"We do not know," the disciples yelled out to the stranger. The man was far away, so they could not see that he was Jesus.

"Drop your net to the other side of the boat," Jesus called to them. "I think you will find some fish there."

The disciples did as the man suggested. When they tried to pull up the net, it was too heavy to lift. The net was full of fish!

"It's a miracle!" they shouted.

Then each disciple looked again to the distant shore. They knew only one man who could perform such a miracle.

"It is Jesus!" Simon Peter cried. "He has come back to us!"

The disciples rowed toward the shore. Simon Peter could not wait for the oars to move the heavy fishing boat. He jumped into the sea and swam to the shore.

"Peace be with you!" Jesus called.

His disciples, amazed and overjoyed, gathered around him. Only days before, they had taken his body to the tomb. Now Jesus stood before them, showing them the marks on his hands and his side.

"It is true! It is you!" they said. "You have returned to us!"

Jesus said to them, "My Father has sent me to you. I bring you the Holy Spirit and its power of forgiveness."

Jesus held up his hands in a blessing. "You will be my messengers, bringing the forgiving power of the Holy Spirit to the world," he said. "Tell everyone that I returned to you and you saw me return to my Father in heaven. Now go to Jerusalem, where I will send you a gift."

With his arms still lifted, Jesus rose into a cloud.

JESUS WILL RETURN

Adapted by Lora Kalkman

Illustrated by Debbie Pinkney

Jesus rose up, up, up into the sky. The disciples could hardly believe their eyes! Soon, all they could see were clouds.

"It is truly amazing," one disciple cried. "He is gone."

"It looks as if he is hiding behind the clouds," another replied, searching the sky. "But he has simply gone home to his Father."

The disciples stood for a moment staring up toward heaven.

Just then, two angels miraculously appeared next to the disciples. The angels were dressed in white. They smiled at the men. "Why do you stand here looking into the sky?" the angels asked.

The disciples explained what they had seen. They told the angels of the beautiful miracle they had been lucky enough to witness.

"It is truly a miracle!" the angels agreed. "As Jesus explained to you, he has returned to heaven for now. But one day, he will return."

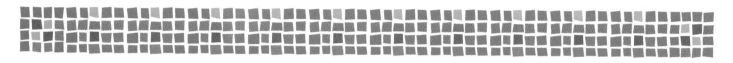

Before Jesus returned to heaven, he had promised his disciples they would receive a gift. He told the men to wait for the gift in Jerusalem, so the good men returned to the city to wait.

In Jerusalem, the disciples went about their daily work. They told as many people as they could about Jesus and his promise to return one day. They also explained that Jesus had promised to send them a gift.

One day, the disciples gathered together to enjoy a meal. It was the day of Pentecost, seven weeks after Jesus had come back to earth after dying on the cross.

As the disciples sat and talked, they heard a loud sound coming from the sky. They thought it might be the wind. When they got up to check, they did not feel the wind blowing. The men were puzzled.

All of a sudden, flames appeared above them. The fire did not burn anything. It seemed to be sending a message, but no one understood what it could mean.

Again, the disciples were puzzled. One opened his mouth to speak. To his surprise, he spoke in a foreign language! In fact, all of the disciples could now speak foreign languages.

The disciples soon realized that they had received the gift that Jesus promised. Because they could now speak in many languages, they could tell everyone they met about Jesus. This was an important gift, because people came to Jerusalem from all over the world to work, to visit, and to pray.

Before Jesus sent his gift, many people could not understand anything the disciples said. The disciples could not understand them either. But now the disciples could speak to people from every country. They could understand everyone's questions, too.

The gift made the disciples very happy. They were excited to tell everybody about their beloved Jesus. With their special gift, they gladly told about his miracles and his love. They could spread Jesus' love across the world.

One day, two disciples named Peter and John were walking through the city. They were going to the temple to pray. Along the way, they stopped to tell people about Jesus.

As they approached the temple gate, they saw a man sitting nearby. He looked sad and hungry. He had a disease and could not walk. He asked Peter and John if they would give him some money to buy a loaf of bread.

"We do not have any money," Peter replied. "But we do have the love of Jesus Christ. Jesus can do anything. He can even make you walk. Stand up and see."

Sure enough, the man rose to his feet and began to walk! He was so happy that he jumped and danced, thanking Jesus for this miracle.

Many people standing nearby witnessed the miracle.

"How did you do that?" a little boy asked Peter.

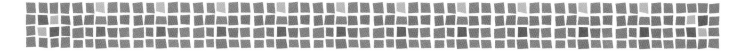

Other people asked questions, too. They were surprised and excited about what they saw. They crowded around Peter and John.

"How can this be?" the people asked. "How can you make a crippled man walk?"

"We did not make this man walk," Peter replied. "Jesus did. Jesus is the Son of God. He can do anything. By making this man walk, Jesus reminds us that he loves us very much."

As Peter talked to the crowd, he saw that many little children had gathered around. Peter remembered that Jesus loved little children most of all.

"Please, sir, will you tell us more about Jesus?" one little boy asked.

Peter smiled and scooped the boy up into his arms. Then he told all of the little children to gather around. Many children came, and Peter spoke to each of them in the language they could understand.

"Jesus loves all people, especially little children," Peter said. "Jesus watches over everyone. You can talk to Jesus anytime you want to."

"But how?" one young girl asked. "How can we talk to Jesus?"

"All you have to do is pray," Peter said with a smile.

He taught the children how to pray. "And remember," Peter told them, "Jesus always hears our prayers."